Black Tickets

"Jayne Anne Phillips is . . . a remarkable new talent. Hers is an authentic and original voice, and her debut [is] just cause for celebration." —*Newsweek*

"Jayne Anne Phillips casts a brilliant, fluorescent light. . . . She is pitiless. She is gifted. She must be read."
—Robie Macauley

"The most exciting young voice in American writing."
—*Newsday*

"The haunting terror of loneliness has rarely been so directly conveyed and with such economy of means. . . . Miss Phillips hears the inner poem—and metaphors explode on every page." —*The New York Times*

"Phillips wonderfully catches the tones and gestures in which familial love unexpectedly persists even after altered circumstances have made it impossible to express directly, and the ways in which grown children, while cherishing even an unrewarding freedom, can be caught and hurt and consoled by their vestigial yearning for dependence, safety, a human closeness that usually seems forever lost."
—*The New York Review of Books*

Books by Jayne Anne Phillips

Black Tickets

Counting

Sweethearts

Machine Dreams

Black Tickets

Jayne Anne Phillips

A LAUREL/SEYMOUR LAWRENCE EDITION

A LAUREL/SEYMOUR LAWRENCE BOOK
Published by
Dell Publishing Co., Inc.
1 Dag Hammarskjold Plaza
New York, New York 10017

ACKNOWLEDGMENTS
   The author would like to thank the National Endowment for the Arts
and the Corporation of Yaddo for their assistance.
   The author wishes to acknowledge that "Souvenir" appeared in *Red-book*, "The Heavenly Animal" in *Fiction International*, and "Happy" in
The Paris Review.
   Some of the stories in this book first appeared in the following publica-
tions: "Wedding Picture" in *New Letters;* "Home" in *The Iowa Review;*
"Sweethearts" and "Under the Boardwalk" in *Truck Magazine;* "Lechery"
in *Persea;* "Gemcrack" and "El Paso" in *Ploughshares;* "1934" in *Canto;*
"Solo Dance" in *North American Review;* "Slave" in *Loka 2;* "Cheers" in
Attaboy; "Snow" in *Fiction;* "Country" (as "Easy") in *Big Deal IV;* "Blind
Girls," "The Powder of the Angels, and I'm Yours," "Stripper," "Stran-
gers in the Night," "What It Takes to Keep a Young Girl Alive," "Satisfac-
tion," and "Accidents" in *Sweethearts;* "Sweethearts," "Under the Boardwalk," and "Blind Girls" appeared in *Pushcart Prize II, Best of the Small
Presses;* "Home" and "Lechery" appeared in *Pushcart Prize IV, Best of
the Small Presses.*
   Lyrics from "Some Enchanted Evening" by Richard Rodgers & Oscar
Hammerstein II: Copyright © 1949 by Richard Rodgers & Oscar Hammer-
stein II. Copyright Renewed. Williamson Music, Inc., owner of publica-
tion and allied rights. International Copyright Secured. All Rights Re-
served. Used by Permission.
   Lyrics from "Ball and Chain" by "Big Momma" Thornton: Bay Tone
Music Publishers and Criesteval Music. Used by Permission.
   Lyrics from "Under the Boardwalk" by Arties Resnick and Kenny
Young: © Copyright 1964 by The Hudson Bay Music Company. Used by
Permission. All Rights Reserved.
   Lyrics from "A Summer Place" by Max Steiner & Mack Discant: © 1964
Warner Bros., Inc. All Rights Reserved. Used by Permission.

Reprinted by arrangement with Delacorte Press/Seymour Lawrence
Printed in the United States of America
First Laurel printing—January 1983
Second Laurel printing—September 1984

Our souls were clean,
but the grass didn't grow.
—Van Morrison
"Streets of Arklow"
from *Veedon Fleece*

Contents

CONTENTS

Black
Tickets

Wedding Picture

My mother's ankles curve from the hem of a white suit as if the bones were water. Under the cloth her body in its olive skin unfolds. The black hair, the porcelain neck, the red mouth that barely shows its teeth. My mother's eyes are round and wide as a light behind her skin burns them to coals. Her heart makes a sound that no one hears. The sound says each fetus floats, an island in the womb.

My father stands beside her in his brown suit and two-tone shoes. He stands also by the plane in New Guinea in 1944. On its side there is a girl on a swing wearing spike heels and short shorts. Her breasts balloon; the sky opens inside them. Yellow hair smooth as a cat's, she is swinging out to him. He glimmers,

blinded by the light. Now his big fingers curl inward. He is trying to hold something.

In her hands the snowy Bible hums, nuns swarming a honeyed cell. The husband is an afterthought. Five years since the
high school lover crumpled on the bathroom floor, his sweet
heart raw. She's twenty-three, her mother's sick, it's time. My
father's heart pounds, a bell in a wrestler's chest. He is almost
forty and the lilies are trumpeting. Rising from his shoulders,
the cross grows pale and loses its arms in their heads.

Home

I'm afraid Walter Cronkite has had it, says Mom. Roger Mudd always does the news now—how would you like to have a name like that? Walter used to do the conventions and a football game now and then. I mean he would sort of appear, on the sidelines. Didn't he? But you never see him anymore. Lord. Something is going on.

Mom, I say. Maybe he's just resting. He must have made a lot of money by now. Maybe he's tired of talking about elections and mine disasters and the collapse of the franc. Maybe he's in love with a young girl.

He's not the type, says my mother. You can tell *that* much. No, she says, I'm afraid it's cancer.

My mother has her suspicions. She ponders. I have been

home with her for two months. I ran out of money and I wasn't in love, so I have come home to my mother. She is an educational administrator. All winter long after work she watches television and knits afghans.

Come home, she said. Save money.

I can't possibly do it, I said. Jesus, I'm twenty-three years old.

Don't be silly, she said. And don't use profanity.

She arranged a job for me in the school system. All day, I tutor children in remedial reading. Sometimes I am so discouraged that I lie on the couch all evening and watch television with her. The shows are all alike. Their laugh tracks are conspicuously similar; I think I recognize a repetition of certain professional laughters. This laughter marks off the half hours.

Finally I make a rule: I won't watch television at night. I will watch only the news, which ends at 7:30. Then I will go to my room and do God knows what. But I feel sad that she sits there alone, knitting by the lamp. She seldom looks up.

Why don't you ever read anything? I ask.

I do, she says. I read books in my field. I read all day at work, writing those damn proposals. When I come home I want to relax.

Then let's go to the movies.

I don't want to go to the movies. Why should I pay money to be upset or frightened?

But feeling something can teach you. Don't you want to learn anything?

I'm learning all the time, she says.

She keeps knitting. She folds yarn the color of cream, the color of snow. She works it with her long blue needles, piercing, returning, winding. Yarn cascades from her hands in long panels. A pattern appears and disappears. She stops and counts;

so many stitches across, so many down. Yes, she is on the right track.

Occasionally I offer to buy my mother a subscription to something mildly informative: *Ms.*, *Rolling Stone*, *Scientific American*.

I don't want to read that stuff, she says. Just save your money. Did you hear Cronkite last night? Everyone's going to need all they can get.

Often, I need to look at my mother's old photographs. I see her sitting in knee-high grass with a white gardenia in her hair. I see her dressed up as the groom in a mock wedding at a sorority party, her black hair pulled back tight. I see her formally posed in her cadet nurse's uniform. The photographer has painted her lashes too lushly, too long; but her deep red mouth is correct.

The war ended too soon. She didn't finish her training. She came home to nurse only her mother and to meet my father at a dance. She married him in two weeks. It took twenty years to divorce him.

When we traveled to a neighboring town to buy my high school clothes, my mother and I would pass a certain road that turned off the highway and wound to a place I never saw.

There it is, my mother would say. The road to Wonder Bar. That's where I met my Waterloo. I walked in and he said, 'There she is. I'm going to marry that girl.' Ha. He sure saw me coming.

Well, I asked, Why did you marry him?

He was older, she said. He had a job and a car. And Mother was so sick.

My mother doesn't forget her mother.

Never one bedsore, she says. I turned her every fifteen minutes. I kept her skin soft and kept her clean, even to the end.

I imagine my mother at twenty-three; her black hair, her
dark eyes, her olive skin and that red lipstick. She is growing
lines of tension in her mouth. Her teeth press into her lower lip
as she lifts the woman in the bed. The woman weighs no more
than a child. She has a smell. My mother fights it continually;
bathing her, changing her sheets, carrying her to the bathroom
so the smell can be contained and flushed away. My mother will
try to protect them both. At night she sleeps in the room on a
cot. She struggles awake feeling something press down on her
and suck her breath: the smell. When my grandmother can no
longer move, my mother fights it alone.

I did all I could, she sighs. And I was glad to do it. I'm glad I
don't have to feel guilty.

No one has to feel guilty, I tell her.

And why not? says my mother. There's nothing wrong with
guilt. If you are guilty, you should feel guilty.

My mother has often told me that I will be sorry when she is
gone.

I think. And read alone at night in my room. I read those
books I never read, the old classics, and detective stories. I can
get them in the library here. There is only one bookstore; it
sells mostly newspapers and *True Confessions* oracles. At
Kroger's by the checkout counter I buy a few paperbacks, best
sellers, but they are usually bad.

The television drones on downstairs.

I wonder about Walter Cronkite.

When was the last time I saw him? It's true his face was

pouchy, his hair thinning. Perhaps he is only cutting it shorter. But he had that look about the eyes—

He was there when they stepped on the moon. He forgot he was on the air and he shouted, 'There . . . there . . . now—We have Contact!' Contact. For those who tuned in late, for the periodic watchers, he repeated: 'One small step . . .'

I was in high school and he was there with the body count. But he said it in such a way that you knew he wanted the war to end. He looked directly at you and said the numbers quietly. Shame, yes, but sorrowful patience, as if all things had passed before his eyes. And he understood that here at home, as well as in starving India, we would pass our next lives as meager cows.

My mother gets *Reader's Digest*. I come home from work, have a cup of coffee, and read it. I keep it beside my bed. I read it when I am too tired to read anything else. I read about Joe's kidney and Humor in Uniform. Always, there are human interest stories in which someone survives an ordeal of primal terror. Tonight it is Grizzly! Two teen-agers camping in the mountains are attacked by a bear. Sharon is dragged over a mile, unconscious. She is a good student loved by her parents, an honest girl loved by her boyfriend. Perhaps she is not a virgin; but in her heart, she is virginal. And she lies now in the furred arms of a beast. The grizzly drags her quietly, quietly. He will care for her all the days of his life . . . Sharon, his rose.

But alas. Already, rescuers have organized. Mercifully, her boyfriend is not among them. He is sleeping en route to the nearest hospital; his broken legs have excused him. In a few days, Sharon will bring him his food on a tray. She is spared. She is not demure. He gazes on her face, untouched but for a

long thin scar near her mouth. Sharon says she remembers
nothing of the bear. She only knows the tent was ripped open,
that its heavy canvas fell across her face.

I turn out my light when I know my mother is sleeping. By
then my eyes hurt and the streets of the town are deserted.

My father comes to me in a dream. He kneels beside me,
touches my mouth. He turns my face gently toward him.

Let me see, he says. Let me see it.

He is looking for a scar, a sign. He wears only a towel around
his waist. He presses himself against my thigh, pretending solic-
itude. But I know what he is doing; I turn my head in repul-
sion and stiffen. He smells of a sour musk and his forearms are
black with hair. I think to myself, It's been years since he's had
an erection—

Finally he stands. Cover yourself, I tell him.

I can't, he says, I'm hard.

On Saturdays I go to the Veterans of Foreign Wars rummage
sales. They are held in the drafty basement of a church, rows of
collapsible tables piled with objects. Sometimes I think I recognize the possessions of old friends: a class ring, yearbooks, football sweaters with our high school insignia. Would this one have
fit Jason?

He used to spread it on the seat of the car on winter nights
when we parked by country churches and graveyards. There
seemed to be no ground, just water, a rolling, turning, building
to a dull pain between my legs.

What's wrong? he said, What is it?

Jason, I can't . . . This pain—

It's only because you're afraid. If you'd let me go ahead—

I'm not afraid of you, I'd do anything for you. But Jason, why does it hurt like this?

We would try. But I couldn't. We made love with our hands. Our bodies were white. Out the window of the car, snow rose up in mounds across the fields. Afterward, he looked at me peacefully, sadly.

I held him and whispered, Soon, soon . . . we'll go away to school.

His sweater. He wore it that night we drove back from the football awards banquet. Jason made All-State but he hated football.

I hate it, he said. So what? he said, that I'm out there puking in the heat? Screaming 'Kill' at a sandbag?

I held his award in my lap, a gold man frozen in midleap. Don't play in college, I said. Refuse the money.

He was driving very slowly.

I can't see, he said, I can't see the edges of the road . . . Tell me if I start to fall off.

Jason, what do you mean?

He insisted I roll down the window and watch the edge. The banks of the road were gradual, sloping off into brush and trees on either side. White lines at the edge glowed up in dips and turns.

We're going to crash, he said.

No, Jason. You've driven this road before. We won't crash.

We're crashing, I know it, he said. Tell me, tell me I'm OK—

Here on the rummage sale table, there are three football sweaters. I see they are all too small to have belonged to Jason. So I buy an old soundtrack, *The Sound of Music*. Air, Austrian mountains. And an old robe to wear in the mornings. It upsets my mother to see me naked; she looks at me so curiously, as though she didn't recognize my body.

I pay for my purchases at the cash register. Behind the desk I glimpse stacks of *Reader's Digests*. The Ladies Auxiliary turns them inside out, stiffens and shellacs them. They make waste-baskets out of them.

I give my mother the record. She is pleased. She hugs me.

Oh, she says, I used to love the musicals. They made me happy. Then she stops and looks at me.

Didn't you do this? she says. Didn't you do this in high school?

Do what?

Your class, she says. You did *The Sound of Music*.

Yes, I guess we did.

What a joke. I was the beautiful countess meant to marry Captain von Trapp before innocent Maria stole his heart. Jason was a threatening Nazi colonel with a bit part. He should have sung the lead but sports practices interfered with rehearsals. Tall, blond, aged in makeup under the lights, he encouraged sympathy for the bad guys and overshadowed the star. He appeared just often enough to make the play ridiculous.

My mother sits in the blue chair my father used for years.

Come quick, she says. Look—

She points to the television. Flickerings of Senate chambers, men in conservative suits. A commentator drones on about tax rebates.

There, says my mother. Hubert Humphrey. Look at him.

It's true. Humphrey is different, changed from his former toady self to a desiccated old man, not unlike the discarded shell of a locust. Now he rasps into the microphone about the people of these great states.

Old Hubert's had it, says my mother. He's a death mask.

That's what he gets for sucking blood for thirty years.

No, she says. No, he's got it too. Look at him! Cancer. Oh.

For God's sake, will you think of something else for once?

I don't know what you mean, she says. She goes on knitting.

All Hubert needs, I tell her, is a good roll in the hay.

You think that's what everyone needs.

Everyone does need it.

They do not. People aren't dogs. I seem to manage perfectly well without it, don't I?

No, I wouldn't say that you do.

Well, I do. I know your mumbo jumbo about sexuality. Sex is for those who are married, and I wouldn't marry again if it was the Lord himself.

Now she is silent. I know what's coming.

Your attitude will make you miserable, she says. One man after another. I just want you to be happy.

I do my best.

That's right, she says. Be sarcastic.

I refuse to answer. I think about my growing bank account. Graduate school, maybe in California. Hawaii. Somewhere beautiful and warm. I will wear few clothes and my skin will feel the air.

What about Jason, says my mother. I was thinking of him the other day.

Our telepathy always frightens me. Telepathy and beyond. Before her hysterectomy, our periods often came on the same day.

If he hadn't had that nervous breakdown, she says softly, do you suppose—

No, I don't suppose.

I wasn't surprised that it happened. When his brother was killed, that was hard. But Jason was so self-centered. You're lucky the two of you split up. He thought everyone was out to get him. Still, poor thing.

Silence. Then she refers in low tones to the few months Jason and I lived together before he was hospitalized.

You shouldn't have done what you did when you went off to college. He lost respect for you.

It wasn't respect for me he lost—He lost his fucking mind if you remember—

I realize I'm shouting. And shaking. What is happening to me?

My mother stares.

We'll not discuss it, she says.

She gets up. I hear her in the bathroom. Water running into the tub. Hydrotherapy. I close my eyes and listen. Soon, this weekend. I'll get a ride to the university a few hours away and look up an old lover. I'm lucky. They always want to sleep with me. For old time's sake.

I turn down the sound of the television and watch its silent pictures. Jason's brother was a musician; he taught Jason to play the pedal steel. A sergeant in uniform delivered the message two weeks before the State Play-Off games. Jason appeared at my mother's kitchen door with the telegram. He looked at me, opened his mouth, backed off wordless in the dark. I pretend I hear his pedal steel; its sweet country whine might make me cry. And I recognize this silent movie—I've seen it four times. Gregory Peck and his submarine crew escape fallout in Australia, but not for long. The cloud is coming. And so they run rampant in auto races and love affairs. But in the end, they close the hatch and put out to sea. They want to go home to die.

Sweetheart? my mother calls from the bathroom. Could you bring me a towel?

Her voice is quavering slightly. She is sorry. But I never know what part of it she is sorry about. I get a towel from the linen closet and open the door of the steamy bathroom. My mother stands in the tub, dripping, shivering a little. She is so small and thin; she is smaller than I. She has two long scars on her belly, operations of the womb, and one breast is misshapen, sunken, indented near the nipple.

I put the towel around her shoulders and my eyes smart. She looks at her breast.

Not too pretty is it, she says. He took out too much when he removed that lump—

Mom, it doesn't look so bad.

I dry her back, her beautiful back which is firm and unblemished. Beautiful, her skin. Again, I feel the pain in my eyes.

But you should have sued the bastard, I tell her. He didn't give a shit about your body.

We have an awkward moment with the towel when I realize I can't touch her any longer. The towel slips down and she catches it as one end dips into the water.

Sweetheart, she says. I know your beliefs are different than mine. But have patience with me. You'll just be here a few more months. And I'll always stand behind you. We'll get along.

She has clutched the towel to her chest. She is so fragile, standing there, naked, with her small shoulders. Suddenly I am horribly frightened.

Sure, I say, I know we will.

I let myself out of the room.

Sunday my mother goes to church alone. Daniel calls me from D.C. He's been living with a lover in Oregon. Now he is

back East; she will join him in a few weeks. He is happy, he
says. I tell him I'm glad he's found someone who appreciates
him.

Come on now, he says. You weren't that bad.

I love Daniel, his white and feminine hands, his thick chestnut hair, his intelligence. And he loves me, though I don't know
why. The last few weeks we were together I lay beside him like
a piece of wood. I couldn't bear his touch; the moisture his
penis left on my hips as he rolled against me. I was cold, cold. I
huddled in blankets away from him.

I'm sorry, I said. Daniel, I'm sorry please—what's wrong with
me? Tell me you love me anyway . . .

Yes, he said, Of course I do. I always will. I do.

Daniel says he has no car, but he will come by bus. Is there a
place for him to stay?

Oh yes, I say. There's a guest room. Bring some Trojans. I'm
a hermit with no use for birth control. Daniel, you don't know
what it's like here.

I don't care what it's like. I want to see you.

Yes, I say. Daniel, hurry.

When he arrives the next weekend, we sit around the table
with my mother and discuss medicine. Daniel was a medic in
Vietnam. He smiles at my mother. She is charmed though she
has reservations; I see them in her face. But she enjoys having
someone else in the house, a presence; a male. Daniel's laughter is low and modulated. He talks softly, smoothly: a dignified
radio announcer, an accomplished anchorman.

But when I lived with him, he threw dishes against the wall.
And jerked in his sleep, mumbling. And ran out of the house
with his hands across his eyes.

After we first made love, he smiled and pulled gently away
from me. He put on his shirt and went to the bathroom. I followed and stepped into the shower with him. He faced me,

composed, friendly, and frozen. He stood as though guarding something behind him.

Daniel, turn around. I'll soap your back.

I already did.

Then move, I'll stand in the water with you.

He stepped carefully around me.

Daniel, what's wrong? Why won't you turn around?

Why should I?

I'd never seen him with his shirt off. He'd never gone swimming with us, only wading, alone, down Point Reyes Beach. He wore long-sleeved shirts all summer in the California heat.

Daniel, I said, You've been my best friend for months. We could have talked about it.

He stepped backwards, awkwardly, out of the tub and put his shirt on.

I was loading them on copters, he told me. The last one was dead anyway; he was already dead. But I went after him, dragged him in the wind of the blades. Shrapnel and napalm caught my arms, my back. Until I fell, I thought it was the other man's blood in my hands.

They removed most of the shrapnel, did skin grafts for the burns. In three years since, Daniel made love five times; always in the dark. In San Francisco he must take off his shirt for a doctor; tumors have grown in his scars. They bleed through his shirt, round rust-colored spots.

Face-to-face in bed, I tell him I can feel the scars with my fingers. They are small knots on his skin. Not large, not ugly. But he can't let me, he can't let anyone, look: he says he feels wild, like raging, and then he vomits. But maybe, after they remove the tumors— Each time they operate, they reduce the scars.

We spend hours at the veterans' hospital waiting for appointments. Finally they schedule the operation. I watch the black-ringed wall clock, the amputees gliding by in chairs that tick on the linoleum floor. Daniel's doctors curse about lack of supplies; they bandage him with gauze and layers of Band-Aids. But it is all right. I buy some real bandages. Every night I cleanse his back with a sponge and change them.

In my mother's house, Daniel seems different. He has shaved his beard and his face is too young for him. I can only grip his hands.

I show him the house, the antiques, the photographs on the walls. I tell him none of the objects move; they are all cemented in place. Now the bedrooms, my room.

This is it, I say. This is where I kept my Villager sweaters when I was seventeen, and my dried corsages. My cups from the Tastee Freeze labeled with dates and boy's names.

The room is large, blue. Baseboards and wood trim are painted a spotless white. Ruffled curtains, ruffled bedspread. The bed itself is so high one must climb into it. Daniel looks at the walls, their perfect blue and white.

It's a piece of candy, he says.

Yes, I say, hugging him, wanting him.

What about your mother?

She's gone to meet friends for dinner. I don't think she believes what she says, she's only being my mother. It's all right.

We take off our clothes and press close together. But something is wrong. We keep trying. Daniel stays soft in my hands. His mouth is nervous; he seems to gasp at my lips.

He says his lover's name. He says they aren't seeing other people.

But I'm not other people. And I want you to be happy with her.

I know. She knew . . . I'd want to see you.

Then what?

This room, he says. This house. I can't breathe in here.

I tell him we have tomorrow. He'll relax. And it is so good just to see him, a person from my life.

So we only hold each other, rocking.

Later, Daniel asks about my father.

I don't see him, I say. He told me to choose.

Choose what?

Between them.

My father. When he lived in this house, he stayed in the dark with his cigarette. He sat in his blue chair with the lights and television off, smoking. He made little money; he said he was self-employed. He was sick. He grew dizzy when he looked up suddenly. He slept in the basement. All night he sat reading in the bathroom. I'd hear him walking up and down the dark steps at night. I lay in the dark and listened. I believed he would strangle my mother, then walk upstairs and strangle me. I believed we were guilty; we had done something terrible to him.

Daniel wants me to talk.

How could she live with him, I ask. She came home from work and got supper. He ate it, got up and left to sit in his chair. He watched the news. We were always sitting there, looking at his dirty plates. And I wouldn't help her. She should wash them, not me. She should make the money we lived on. I didn't want her house and his ghost with its cigarette burning in the dark like a sore. I didn't want to be guilty. So she did it. She sent me to college; she paid for my safe escape.

Daniel and I go to the Rainbow, a bar and grill on Main Street. We hold hands, play country songs on the jukebox, drink a lot of salted beer. We talk to the barmaid and kiss in the overstuffed booth. Twinkle lights blink on and off above us. I

wore my burgundy stretch pants in here when I was twelve.
senior pinched me, then moved his hand slowly across m
thigh, mystified, as though erasing the pain.

What about tonight? Daniel asks. Would your mother go ou
with us? A movie? A bar? He sees me in her, he likes her. He
wants to know her.

Then we will have to watch television.

We pop popcorn and watch the late movies. My mother stay
up with us, mixing whiskey sours and laughing. She gets a high
color in her cheeks and the light in her eyes glimmers up; she i
slipping, slipping back and she is beautiful, oh, in her ankle
socks, her red mouth and her armor of young girl's common
sense. She has a beautiful laughter. She and Daniel end by
mock arm wrestling; he pretends defeat and goes upstairs to
bed.

My mother hears his door close. He's nice, she says. You've
known some nice people, haven't you?

I want to make her back down.

Yes, he's nice, I say. And don't you think he respects me?
Don't you think he truly cares for me, even though we've slep
together?

He seems to, I don't know. But if you give them that, it cost
them nothing to be friends with you.

Why should it cost? The only cost is what you give, and you
can tell if someone is giving it back.

How? How can you tell? By going to bed with every man you
take a fancy to?

I wish I took a fancy oftener, I tell her. I wish I wanted more
I can be good to a man, but I'm afraid—I can't be physical, no
really . . .

You shouldn't.

I should. I want to, for myself as well. I don't think—I've ever had an orgasm.

What? she says, Never? Haven't you felt a sort of building up, and then a dropping off . . . a conclusion? like something's over?

No, I don't think so.

You probably have, she assures me. It's not necessarily an explosion. You were just thinking too hard, you think too much.

But she pauses.

Maybe I don't remember right, she says. It's been years, and in the last years of the marriage I would have died if your father had touched me. But before, I know I felt something. That's partly why I haven't . . . since . . . what if I started wanting it again? Then it would be hell.

But you have to try to get what you want—

No, she says. Not if what you want would ruin everything. And now, anyway. Who would want me?

I stand at Daniel's door. The fear is back; it has followed me upstairs from the dead dark bottom of the house. My hands are shaking. I'm whispering . . . Daniel, don't leave me here.

I go to my room to wait. I must wait all night, or something will come in my sleep. I feel its hands on me now, dragging, pulling. I watch the lit face of the clock: three, four, five. At seven I go to Daniel. He sleeps with his pillow in his arms. The high bed creaks as I get in. Please now, yes . . . he is hard. He always woke with erections . . . inside me he feels good, real, and I tell him no, stop, wait . . . I hold the rubber, stretch its rim away from skin so it smooths on without hurting and fills with him . . . now again, here, yes but quiet, be quiet . . . oh

Daniel . . . the bed is making noise . . . yes, no, but be careful, she . . . We move and turn and I forget about the sounds. We push against each other hard, he is almost there and I am almost with him and just when it is over I think I hear my mother in the room directly under us—But I am half dreaming. I move to get out of bed and Daniel holds me. No, he says, stay.

We sleep and wake to hear the front door slam.

Daniel looks at me.

There's nothing to be done, I say. She's gone to church.

He looks at the clock. I'm going to miss that bus, he says. We put our clothes on fast and Daniel moves to dispose of the rubber—how? the toilet, no, the wastebasket—He drops it in, bends over, retrieves it. Finally he wraps it in a Kleenex and puts it in his pocket. Jesus, he swears. He looks at me and grins. When I start laughing, my eyes are wet.

I take Daniel to the bus station and watch him out of sight. I come back and strip the bed, bundle the sheets in my arms. This pressure in my chest . . . I have to clutch the sheets tight, tighter—

A door clicks shut. I go downstairs to my mother. She refuses to speak or let me near her. She stands by the sink and holds her small square purse with both hands. The fear comes. I hug myself, press my hands against my arms to stop shaking. My mother runs hot water, soap, takes dishes from the drainer. She immerses them, pushes them down, rubbing with a rag in a circular motion.

Those dishes are clean, I tell her. I washed them last night.

She keeps washing. Hot water clouds her glasses, the window in front of us, our faces. We all disappear in steam. I watch the dishes bob and sink. My mother begins to sob. I move close to her and hold her. She smells as she used to smell when I was a child and slept with her.

I heard you, I heard it, she says. Here, in my own house. Please, how much can you expect me to take? I don't know what to do about anything . . .

She looks into the water, keeps looking. And we stand here just like this.

Blind
Girls

She knew it was only boys in the field, come to watch them drunk on first wine. A radio in the little shack poured out promises of black love and lips. Jesse watched Sally paint her hair with grenadine, dotting the sticky syrup on her arms. The party was in a shack down the hill from her house, beside a field of tall grass where black snakes lay like flat belts. The Ripple bottles were empty and Jesse told pornographic stories about various adults while everyone laughed; about Miss Hicks the home-ec teacher whose hands were dimpled and moist and always touching them. It got darker and the stories got scarier. Finally she told their favorite, the one about the girl and her boyfriend parked on a country road. On a night like this with the wind blowing and then rain, the whole sky sobbing pota juice. Please let's leave, pleads girlie, It sounds like something scratching at the car. For God's sake, grumbles boyfriend, and takes off squealing. At home they find the hook of a crazed amputee caught in the door. Jesse described his yellow face, putrid, and his blotchy stump. She described him panting in the grass, crying and looking for something. She could feel him smelling of raw vegetables, a rejected bleeding cowboy with wheat hair, and she was unfocused. Moaning in the dark and falsetto voices. Don't don't please don't. Nervous laughter. Sally looked out the window of the shack. The grass is moving, she said, Something's crawling in it. No, it's nothing. Yes, there's something coming, and her voice went up at the end. It's just boys trying to scare us. But Sally whined and flailed her arms. On her knees she hugged Jesse's legs and mumbled into her thighs. It's all right, I'll take you up to the house. Sally was stiff, her nails digging the skin. She wouldn't move. Jesse tied a scarf around her eyes and led her like a horse through fire up the hill to the house, one poison light soft in a window. Boys ran out of the field squawling.

Lechery

Though I have no money I must give myself what I need. Yes I know which lovers to call when the police have caught me peddling pictures, the store detectives twisting my wrists pull stockings out of my sleeves. And the butchers pummel the small of my back to dislodge their wrapped hocks; white bone and marbled tendon exposed as the paper tears and they push me against the wall. They curse me, I call my lovers. I'm nearly fifteen, my lovers get older and older. I know which ones will look at me delightedly, pay my bail, take me home to warm whiskey and bed. I might stay with them all day; I might run as the doors of their big cars swing open. Even as I run I can hear them behind me, laughing.

* * *

I go down by the schools with my pictures. The little boy
smoke cigarettes, they're girlish as faggots, they try to ac
tough. Their Camels are wrinkled from pockets, a little chewed
I imagine them wet and stained pinkish at the tips, pink from
their pouty lips. The boys have tight little chests, I see har
nipples in their T-shirts. Lines of smooth stomach, little peni
tucked into jockey briefs. Already they're growing shaggy hai
and quirky curves around their smiles. But no acne, I get then
before they get pimples, I get them those first few times th
eyes flutter and get strange. I show them what I do. Five or si
surround me, jingling coins, tapping toes in tennis shoes.
know they've got some grade-school basketball coach, some ex
jock with a beer gut and a hard-on under his sweat pants in th
locker room; that kills me. They come closer, I'm watching th
ridged toes of their shoes. Now I do it with my eyes, I look u
and pick the one I want. I tell him to collect the money an
meet me at lunch in a park across the street, in a culvert, in
soft ditch, in a car parked under a bridge or somewhere shaded
Maybe I show them a few pills. One picture; blowsy redhea
with a young blond girl, the girl a kneeling eunuch on whit
knees. The redhead has good legs, her muscles stand out tense
and she comes standing up. I tell them about it. Did you eve
come standing up. I ask them, they shift their eyes at eac
other. I know they've been in blankets in dark bedrooms, se
who can beat off first. Slapping sounds and a dry urge. But the
don't understand their soft little cocks all stiff when they wak
up in daylight, how the bed can float around.

So at noon I wait for them. I don't smoke, it's filthy. I suck
smooth pebble and wait. I've brushed my teeth in a gas station
I press my lips with my teeth and suck them, make them soft
Press dots of oil to my neck, my hands. Ambergris or musk be

tween my breasts, down in the shadowed place where hair starts in a line at my groin. Maybe I brush my hair. I let them see me do it, open a compact and tongue my lips real slow. They only see the soft tip of my tongue, I pretend it's not for them.

Usually just one of them comes, the one I chose, with a friend waiting out of sight where he can see us. If they came alone I can tell by looking at them. Sometimes they are high on something, I don't mind. Maybe I have them in an abandoned car down in a back lot, blankets on the seat or no back seat but an old mattress. Back windows covered up with paper sacks and speckled mud, sun through dirty windows or brown paper makes the light all patterns.

He is nervous. Right away he holds out the money. Or he is a little mean, he punches at me with his childish fist. A fine blond boy with a sweet neck and thin collarbones arched out like wings, or someone freckled whose ashen hair falls loose. A dark boy, thick lashes and cropped wooled hair, rose lips full and swelling a little in the darkened car. I give him a little whiskey, rifle through the pictures and pretend to arrange them. I take a drink too, joke with him. This is my favorite time; he leans back against the seat with something like sleep in his eyes. I stroke his hard thighs, his chest, I comfort him.

I put the pictures beside us, some of them are smaller than postcards. We put our faces close to see them. A blond girl, a black girl, they like to see the girls. One bending back droops her white hair while the other arches over, holds her at the waist, puts her mouth to a breast so small only the nipple stands up. In the picture her mouth moves in and out, anyone can tell.

black hand nearly touching pale pubic hair, a forefinger al-

most tender curls just so, moves toward a slit barely visible just
below the pelvic bone. I don't like pictures of shaven girls, it
scares them to see so much. It makes them disappear.

I do things they've never seen, I could let them touch but no
I arrange their hands and feet, keep them here forever. Some
times they tell me stories, they keep talking of baseball games
and vicious battles with their friends. Lips pouty and soft, eyes
a hard glass glitter. They lose the words and mumble like ba
bies; I hold them just so, just tight, I sing the oldest songs. A
times their smooth faces seem to grow smaller and smaller in
my vision. I concentrate on their necks, their shoulders. Loosen
their clothes and knead their scalps, pinching hard at the base
of the head. Maybe that boy with dark hair and Spanish skin
his eyes flutter, I pull him across my legs and open his shirt
Push his pants down to just above his knees so his thin legs and
smooth cock are exposed; our breathing is wavy and thick, we
make a sound like music. He can't move his legs but stiffens in
my lap, palms of his hands turned up. In a moment he will roll
his eyes and come, I'll gently force my coated fingers into his
mouth. I'll take off my shirt and rub my slick palms around my
breasts until the nipples stand up hard and frothy. I force his
mouth to them. I move my hand to the tight secret place be
tween his buttocks. Sometimes they get tears in their eyes.

In the foster homes they used to give me dolls and I played
the church game. At first I waited till everyone left the house
Then it didn't matter who was around. I lined up all the dolls on
the couch, I sat them one after the other. They were ugly, most
of them had no clothes or backward arms. They were dolls from
the trash, the Salvation Army at Christmas, junk-sale dolls. On
of them was in a fire. The plastic hand was missing, melted into

a bubbled fountain dribbling in nubs down the arm. We faced the front of the room. I made us sit for hours unmoving, listening to nothing at all and watching someone preach.

Uncle Wumpy gave me a doll. They call him that. Like his pocked face had rabbit ears and soft gray flesh. His face is pitted with tiny scars, his skin is flushed. We won at the carnival: cowboy hats, a rubber six-gun, a stuffed leopard with green diamond eyes for Kitty. We were on our way out between booths and machines, sawdust sticky with old candy and beer, to pick Kitty up at work. We passed the duckshoot. Wumpy was so drunk I had to help him with the gun and we drowned them all. Little yellow ducks with flipped up tail feathers and no eyeballs; they glided by hooked to a string. We hit them, knocked them back with a snap like something breaking. We hit twelve; the whole group popped up, started gliding by again as eyeless as before. So we kept shooting and shooting . . . The barker came out from behind the counter with his fat long-ashed cigar. He held it pinched in two fingers like something dirty he respected. Then he sucked on it and took the gun away. The crowd behind us mumbled. He thrust the doll into my arms. She was nearly three feet tall, pearl earrings, patent leather heels. Long white dress and a veil fastened with a clear plastic bird. I took the bird, I lit it with Wumpy's lighter. Its neck melted down to a curve that held its flat head molded to its wings. I liked to keep the bird where no one saw it. Finally I buried it in a hole, I took it to a place I knew I'd forget.

How I found Wumpy. I was twelve, I lived with Minnie. She made me work in the luncheonette, swab Formica tables with a

rag. Bend over to wipe the aluminum legs, clotted ketchup. By
the grill her frozen french fries thawed out limp and fishy. She
threw them in sooty fat; they fizzled and jumped and came ou
shining. Her old face squinched like a rat's, she was forty. Wore
thick glasses and a red handkerchief on her head, liked the gos
pel shows turned up loud. One hand was twisted. She had the
arthritis, the rheumatism, the corns, the bunions on he
knotted toes as she walked to the shower at home. Hunched in
her long robe, she fixed her eyes on the bathroom door. Scut
tled clinching herself at the waist and slammed the door.

After school I walked to the restaurant and helped her clea
tables till seven. She cursed the miners under her breath
Slapped my butt if I was slow, moved her hard hand, its bi
twisted knuckles. Grabbed the curve of my ass and squeezed.

Wumpy came in every night for coffee. He cut brush for th
State Road Commission. Watched Minnie and me. Kitty starte
coming in with him. Cellophane Baggie full of white crosses
cheap speed. She'd order a Pepsi, take a few pills, grind a fe
more to powder on the tabletop. She winked, gave me hair rib
bons, said she'd like to take me to the movies. Wumpy tol
Minnie I needed some clothes, he and Kitty would take me t
Pittsburgh to buy me some dresses. They gave her thirty do
lars.

In the motel I stood in the bathroom and vomited. Sopor
floated in the bowl, clumps of white undissolved powder in
clear mucus. I puked so easy, again and again, I almost laughe
Then they came in naked and took off my clothes. I couldn
stand up, they carried me to the bed. Wumpy got behind he
and fucked her, she kept saying words but I couldn't keep m
eyes open. She pulled me down She said Honey Honey. In th
bottom of something dark I rocked and rocked. His big arm
put me there until he lifted me. Lifted me held my hips in th
air and I felt her mouth on my legs, I felt bigger and bigge

he ceiling spun around like the lights at Children's Center
pun in the dark halls when I woke up at night. Then a tight
nuscular flash, I curled up and hugged myself.

I stood by the window and fingered the flimsy curtains. I
vatched them sleeping, I didn't leave. I watched Wumpy's
road back rising and falling.

Wumpy would never do it to me, he gave me pictures to sell.
wanted to give him the money, he laughed at me. He had
ttle stars in the flesh of his hands. He took me to bars. We
ook a man to some motel, Wumpy said he always had to watch
. . stood by the bed while I choked and gagged a little, salt
xploding in my throat—

The dream is here again and again, the dream is still here.
Natalie made the dream. I slept with her when I was eight, six
nonths we slept together. She whimpered at night, she wet the
ed. Both of us wards of the state, they got money for us. Cold
the bedroom, she wrapping her skinny arms around my
nest. Asking can she look at me. But I fall asleep, I won't take
ff my clothes in bed with her. I fall asleep and the same dream
omes.

Natalie is standing in the sand. Behind her the ocean spills
ver, the waves have thick black edges. Natalie in her shredded
ip, knobby knees, her pale blue eyes all watery. Natalie standing
ill as a dead thing spreads her legs and holds herself with her
and. Her fingers groping, her white face. She squeezes and
ulls so hard she bleeds She calls for help She wants me. Faces
around us, big faces just teeth and lips to hold me down for

Natalie. Natalie on top of me Natalie pressing down. Her wa
tery eyes say nothing. She sighs with pleasure and her hot urin
boils all around us.

I remember like this: Natalie watches me all the time
They're gone all day, we stay alone with the silent baby. Onc
there's no food but a box of salt. Bright blue box, the silve
spout pops out. The girl with the umbrella dimples and swing
her pony tails, flashes her white skin. I can eat it Natalie. I ca
eat it all. She looks out the window at the snow. I know she
scared. I sit down on the floor at her feet. The box is round lil
a tom-tom, I tip it up. Salt comes in my mouth so fast, fills m
up but I can't quit pouring it . . . I start to strangle but Natal
won't look, she screams and screams. She kicks at me with he
bare blue feet, the box flies across the room throwing fans
salt. When it gets dark, salt gleams on the floor with a strang
cool light. Natalie stays in her chair without moving and I get
sleep alone.

I got lavish cards at Children's Center, I think a jokester se
them. To Daughter From Mother At Christmas, scrolls
stand-up gold and velvet poinsettias. I used to think about tl
janitors, those high school boys with smirky eyes and be
breath, licking the envelopes . . . somehow mailing them fro
Wichita or Tucson. The agency moved me from home to hom
Holidays I stayed at the center, they did paper work to pla
me again. Every time there was a different pasty-faced boy wi
ragged nails, dragging a dun-colored mop. The cards came, th
were never quite right. When I was ten, For Baby's Fir
Christmas—a fold-out hobbyhorse, a mommy with blond h
and popped eyes. I was seven, the card said Debutante

raised silver script, showed a girl in mink and heels. After I
started getting arrested the psychiatrist told them to hold my
mail. They said I might go to an asylum.

Baby Girl Approximately 14 Months Abandoned December
1960, Diagnosed As Mute. But when I was three I made sounds
like trucks and wasps, I screamed and sang. They think I'm
crazy, this is what happens—

I like to lock the bathroom door late at night. Stand in front of
the mirrors, hold a candle under my chin. Stare at my shadowed face and see the white shape of a skull. I lay down on the
cold tile floor and do it to myself by the stalls. I do it, I lay on
my stomach. Hold my breath, riding on the heels of my hands
I'm blind; I feel the hush hush of water pipes through the floor.
Ride up over a hump into the heat the jangling it holds me.
When I open my eyes and roll over, the ceiling is very high it is
the color of bone, lamplight through the barred windows. I
make myself good I do it. Lay on the cold floor, its tiny geomet-
ric blocks. My skin goes white as porcelain, I'm big as the old
sinks and toilets, the empty white tubs. White glass, marble,
rock, old pipes bubbling air. When those white streaks flash in
my vision I run here. I watch her. I know she is me. She runs
from stall to stall flushing toilets, she does it again and again.
Slushing water louder and louder, then high-pitched wail of the
tanks filling. Crash and wail. I crouch on the floor and listen. I
don't let anyone in.

I think Natalie is dead, she said she would die when she was
twelve. But only then. In August under trees we sat heaving
rocks. She buried her feet in sand and said she was a stone. I
could pinch her till my nails rimmed with red; if she didn't cry

out I had to do what she said. She wanted to play house again:
I'm a house I'm a giant house. Crawl through my legs Its the
door. And she heaved herself onto my back, cupped my chin in
her hands. Pulled my head back to see her face above me. She
stroked my throat, pointed her pink tongue in my ear and
hissed. Shhhh. Hissing. Shhhhhh. Purring, breathing deep in
her belly. She pretended her voice was a man. I love you
You're mine Eat your food. And I licked her hand all over, up
and down between her fingers.

Once the man came after us. We were in the shed behind the
house. Natalie liked that room with the tools and jugs, rusted
rakes, wood in splintered piles and the squeaking rats. She took
off her clothes, draped them on random nails to make an
armless girl. A man's big black boots swallowed her ankles. She
white and hairless, jingling the metal clasps. Natalie laughing
and laughing. We held the blunt-nosed hammers, we threw
them hard. Indented circles in the floor, piles of circles pressing
down in the old wood like invisible coins. Natalie said we made
money. More and more, on the wall, on the floor. Natalie at the
windows crashing, glass in glittered piles on her shiny black
rubber boots.

He opens the creaky door. What the hell are you doing. I
hide by the workbench, back in the webs and spiders. The un-
buckling, quick snaky swish of his belt against his pants. He
catches her, throws her over the workbench. Natalie gets quiet,
the big boots fall off her feet. Her feet almost have faces, dangling, alabaster, by my face; her thin white legs hanging down.
Slaps of the belt and drawn-out breathing. You little bitch. He
takes a penny and throws it to shadows in the dust. She knows
She always knows She finds it. Handfuls of clattering coins.
Natalie walks in her goose-pimpled skin, makes a pile of copper
pennies by his shoes. He pushes her down on her knees, Natalie is laughing just a little. I see his back, his wide hips, the

green work pants. Touch it, he says. Natalie says she can't, her
hands are poison.

I'm pure, driven snow. I clean the house, make soup from a
can. Wumpy drinks a beer. Squeezes cans till they buckle and
fold, throws them in a corner. I want to touch him, squeeze him
hard; he closes his eyes to make sounds in his scratchy voice. If
I take off my shirt he hits me. Kitty hugs me, My Baby. She
wants me to do what she wants. Wumpy does what she says.
More and more, she wants what I want. We move around on
the checkerboard floor.

Kitty is on probation. We give her lots of coffee and get her
walking. Every Saturday the parole officer wants her to talk.
Maybe she scores, comes back with smack in an envelope.
Darker and darker, snow feathers down to wrap us up. Kitty
nods out on the windowsill, curls up like a dormer mouse in her
bulky red coat. She likes to lean out almost too far. Wumpy: I
watch him through a lopsided hole in the bathroom door, he
wants to be alone. Ties off, bulges a vein to hit. Hums and
sighs. Pipes make watery yawns and wheezes, they come
together in the tunneled walls. It's so quiet I hear the click of
the neon sign before it changes and throws a splattered word
across the floor. Rooms, it says, blue Rooms. When I see someone move, I'm afraid: If Natalie weren't dead she would find
me.

Mamasita

Mamasita goes out after dark to chase the drunks with a stick. And they stumble up the lighted broken steps of the Men's Social Care Center while the cops laugh at Mamasita. Mamasita hairy and black, drooped red melons in her shirt. Oh Billy Babo you is the plague of your mother, Oh she screams, I will beeet you . . . And she herds them in. To the showers and the tin cups and the hard horned hands of the cops. She squeeze their nuts, they say Oh mama no. She slap, slap, they say Oh yes mama. Mamasita remembers her daddy, falling up and down steps in the Bowery, poison exhale of his breath, gagging and raging his young drunk curses and she a small fat swab in a corner. How the closet, hunker, press, oh press close, where she sat for hours when he forgot where he put her. How she look up, weepy snot, and him big hands reaching down. How the bottles smell. Dark, thick-edged, and the feet drag on another step. Brothers drunk and flashy, young flashy drunks, cut each other up for bangles oh press close. Mamasita long time ago fat and pregnant gets her jaw broke up. But she feel big now, she is big. Till the drunks, the old ones, tell their whimpers in the dark. Their soft mousy sex, such whisper. Bony crouch on newspaper, cornered swabs. Got nothin get nothin. Mamasita hard as nails. They crouch, pick their crabbed groins there by the lamps. Mamasita, oh she goes out with her stick. She likes the ones so gone they don't attack, they don't defend. She feel that soft swab, sniveling girl in her gut, oh she want to kill her. And the frowzy stumblers with their faces cut, with their dank dumb eyes and weighted lids, they look up at Mamasita. Their guts rolled up in tiny balls. Long time ago they roll up their guts, what they got. Got to get somethin mama. Mama. Mamasita with her sausage smell and big stick pouring down. Something ground up, rolled in offal, wrapped in a slick spiced skin. Eat it, eat it up. The pigs roll in their pissed pants up into the light. Because that's how she wants them, that's what she wants.

Black
Tickets

Jamaica Delila, how I want you; your smell a clean yeast, a high white yogurt of the soul. Raymond would be happy to tell me you set me up. He'd say somebody had to lay down, somebody had to sail by, somebody had to do lock-up in this cadillac of castles, and I was the shit-bred pigeon. But Raymond never made it with you in the bathtub (What? you said, Raymond, that moody hunch?), bubbles and wavelets slapping the porcelain sides, soap flowers white on your high mongolian cheeks, your wide-open lavender eyes shadowed with the pale green of a young bruise, your lips mouthing a heavenly O of surprise.

Late at night I think about hitting you. I double my fist and squeeze until the pain makes me tingle. When you fell back on the bed your hair spread out like feathers. I play you over and

over in my head until you're falling so slow the hours pass a
your hands move up to shield your face, tips of your finger
rose-tinged and rounded. I read the lines of your palms that are
lightened in the glow of the lamp. I kept the bedroom near
dark for weeks so that when you walked toward me the tilte
lampshade by the bed threw an ocher glow on your stomach
But before that I lay watching you; you sat in the chair, smokin
and looking at the street. You wore those boy's shirts, like th
ones I wore to school when I was thirteen, button-downs wit
long tails and cuffed sleeves. Or those knit ones, red and green
open-necked, with the tiny alligator sewn on the chest. Golfer'
shirts. I think about your clothes, their detergent and hot wate
smell, about pulling them off in the dark. Your insides wer
muscular, pushing me; it felt like fighting underwater. Yo
liked to be held for a long time with your clothes on, grapplin
slow and fast on the bed like teen-agers in a black park with th
night to kill. You were skinny and you felt like a kid in boy
clothes. In my head at night a figment of Raymond tells me yo
still wear those shirts. Does he know about the underpants too
boy's briefs, thick white cotton. You said they felt good, lik
diapers, rubbed the sewn ridge in front and your flatness unde
neath. In bed you drew faces on our legs with a lipstick penci
faces eating chomped cigarettes, thought bubbles with word
above their heads—Harumph! Mmmmmmmmmmm—and face
whose heavy earrings pulled their heads to their shoulder
Then you made them crawl like crabs across you, six legs, side
ways scuttle.

During the day you sat in the ticket booth at Obelisk, ber
nied up and staring at a cardboard wheel, a layered look-alik
procession of inch-long coupons that opened the magical doo
of the oldest movie house in Philly. While the lady schlumpe
walked their shopping bags and weasel-boned spics did music
slides past the window, you got fixed on tickets and watche

them like TV, studied them with a dimestore magnifying glass. You drew them, perfect tickets, on your knees: Obelisk Theatre, C Street, Philadelphia, Murphey Enterprises Inc., set off by a wavery line and numbered: 028949, 028950, 028951 . . . bright orange, that watery bright of crab's shells. And reversed: The management reserves the right to revoke the license granted by this ticket by refunding purchase price. Fuzzy emblem with a centered star, signed S-7, National Ticket Co., Shamaken, PA. You came home with chains of inked-on tickets across your thighs. Geezes, marks, numb doughboys came to the morning shows, dropped inside and pulled their puds to choruses of Nazi blonds while you sat outside behind the glass bubble devising your own tattoos. Like getting fed, you told me, sitting there catching coins as they slid cupped in a wooden curve through the half-moon hole in the bubble. At night there were lots of boys in hats, wop musicians out of gigs, winos looking for a chair. And a few women in boots, aging a bright platinum.

But days were best. Days were OK. I stood across the street watching you and waiting to make the drop. At first it was sideline stuff, Nembies and speed balls, a little white stuff for the joy bangers who came downtown to cop. I bought a ticket from you, threw the money in that cupped slot and saw your fingernails, blackish violet, catch the silver faces of the quarters. I went inside. Obelisk. The bathrooms were big, horsehair sofa and fan-man carpets worn through, then the white tile floors broken and chipped till the border mosaics were cracked to an ivory powder. We used to cut speed with that powder; all those silky Main Line debs reeling in their mommy's sports cars, digesting the crumbling universe of Obelisk. *Some enchanted evening* I whistled old songs *you may see a stranger* and scooped up the finest particles *across a crowded room* by the long mirror. Friendly mirror, old art deco; a serious flamingo

balanced on one straight leg, big sitting ball of sun going down
behind. Urinals rust-stained and scenting out a poison sweet of
piss. Obelisk: reduced by the Puerto Rican neighborhood to
obligatory porn, cracked frontal filigree, and balcony boxes that
could barely support the weight of the rats; cinematic rodents
who dragged off whole boxes of discarded popcorn. In the dark
you could see the white stripes of the boxes moving smoothly in
the corners and along the walls: they had it down to a science.
They came along later between shows, chirping, to clean up the
flowered kernels they'd spilled in their labors. Ah, the Obelisk
rats. How I miss those rangy fuckers. Raymond had fantasies of
training them to make the drops, do our work for us. He said
they weren't ordinary rats; they were wise guys, street smart,
city old, telepathic. And they were vain, living for generations
in the midst of those flaky ornate mirrors and rotted plush seats.
We could pay them in little red hats and silk vests scaled to
size.

Raymond had time to hatch plots, sitting in the coffee shop
across the street and waiting for me to appear with our hard-
earned money. All I needed was a trench coat and a Luger, a
banded felt hat to pull down over my eyes. I complained that it
was all too elementary. Raymond said of course it was elementary, that's why it worked. Perfectly. For months. And Jamaica
was in good with old man Neinmann. Neinmann couldn't back
out; the dicks would never believe we did our biz there all this
time and Neinmann didn't know it. Besides, smiled Raymond,
the old choke had a thing about going back to Germany before
he croaked; he was saving his pennies. Raymond nodded
drumming his fingers and their rippled whitish nails on table
tops, ducking his head, his jacket humped like he had a sweat
shirt wadded up in it. He said he was just a nice Jewish boy
doing his bit for reverse reparations. Reptilian Raymond, slow
speech and cherub mouth, his head darting forward in thos

jerky chin-stretching movements like some tousle-headed turtle. Droopy blue eyes, movie star jaw, Raymond: Quasimodo with the head of an angel, walked with a hesitant lurch and dragged one foot. He said he was, obviously, conspicuous; I would make the drops, he would keep things clean. And Neinmann, that old storm trooper, slouched by the projection booth giving hell in his diluted German rotgut to the Filipino projectionist. Jamaica, you thin wonder in schoolboy clothes, I could crush them all into a burlap bag full of stones and watch them sink in a sewer named for you. Jamaica, like pieces of wood in my bloodstream; turning your head away from me on the street, walking ahead of me up the stairs with your straight shoulders, saying nothing, even your footsteps sounding arrogant, luxurious, secretive; slide of your shoes on worn rubber-treaded steps. I always listened, thought I would find something out and use it. You liked me to use what I knew. Sweet Jamaica, who was never innocent. Each time with you was one more chance to crash through.

Women and stomachs. Here we go nowhere. My cell door is identical to the rest of my wall-with-a-view, and to think my old man broke his ass to put a picture window in his suburban claptrap house. Bungalow, my mother called it. Bungalow, deep in the forest green. Honeymoons and champagne. He rode the train in every day and sat at the fake-maple dinette at night. I wish I could say she diddled the grocery boy, but that was the woman next door. Our esteemed neighbor locked her kid out of the house when the delivery boys came around, and I sat, like a preschool obedience course graduate, with that rejected sniveling bimbo in the back by the scratchy hedges. Inside his mother was having her jollies and my mother did worse; she watched

them with binoculars like the prize champ she was. A charming
3-D view. We bust our balls to start out small and keep moving.
Numberless advancements. Jamaica: the last time I moved up I
got to you, got inside and forgot the rules. Unpardonable infrac-
tion. Admit one, two. Admit where you got your information.
Officer, I got it from the corner machine; multicolored por-
nography individually wrapped. A subtle gradation of desire at
inflated prices. It's obvious I've graduated. Three days here and
the trustee speaks to me; I eat in the courthouse dining hall.
The last time, a county jail in Florida, statutory rape, they let us
out of eight cells into a hallway to eat. Then we lined up and
scraped our leavings into the one toilet, flushed it, watched
burbling chicken bones and mashed potatos engage with green
peas in a smear and gush of water; reminding you of all your
sick vomits in bathrooms of restaurants, theaters, gas stations,
train depots—all of it coinciding in a rush; exactly how it felt,
how it smelled, your head on the bowl, knees on hard floor,
cold sweat of the porcelain, nothing to grab, bird's-eye view, in-
timate stains of countless patrons, high whishy flow of the
plumbing, eight running commodes, drip of the sinks, your feet
sticking out of the stall, occasional footsteps of witnesses cutting
a wide swath . . .

Jamaica, in sickness and in health. I was sick the day you
found me, having hit Philly on the lam after paying off one
greasy Floridian uncle and waving good-bye to underage
cracker girls. I bought your drinks in that bar beside the tene-
ment walk-up and followed you out, got you in the chipped
green doorway of the building, wanted to beat or crush or fuck
that two-day bus ride and week in the southern slam out of my
swollen head. I touched your legs and felt for you through your
clothes, thought from the way you looked, walked, that if I
pressed myself against you and pushed, you'd come back at me.
I knew you wouldn't scream. You reached down and unzipped

me, keys still in your hand, your warm surprising fingers on my balls, tight, and you touched me with the cold metal, pressing; how the breath went out of me and came back in one steely point. You said to step away and follow you upstairs. When you took those keys away to open the door I could have broken your face. Jamaica Delila. Later I forced the name out of you; hearing it like falling into jungle my mother only dreamed about with her bungalow stories pressed between her legs. Jamaica: not the usual dance. You were falling; I could slap you and push you, keep you moving, falling and falling; it was like you hit on your back with a snapping sound and water sprayed all around us. Then you went under; I didn't feel you.

I wake up alone here at night and the guards are playing poker in the hall. I hear the money rolling, touch the ridged bricks of the wall I'm shoved against, have rolled close to like some newborn rattish creature longing for the nearest suckle. I can taste the skin of your arms; I hate you. And when I fall asleep again into the black, the slap of the cards follows me, constant, funereal: slapping engines of driverless hearses long enough to carry the box of the body, and the slapping feet of the men that follow the box. They have no faces and they feel with the whiskers of dogs.

Animal churches, clutch and clutter. Tempo of the vertical beat danced in amyl dreams. Raymond wanted to cash in on the sex quiz; join the rest of them down there at the bottom of the gorge. Boxes of amyl packaged in a gross of drugstore inhalers or small perfume bottles with cork stoppers: items the hipsters

long for. Added attractions, said Raymond, those little extras t
close down the days and promote orgasmic endings: Gene Autr
riding into coral skyline while the cacti stand up ancient an
timeless as Lucifer. Legions of pretty boys loving each other u
to the tune of the late show and spinning off like random pin
balls in the flash of the nitrite wizard. Feel that grand connec
tion coming on and you quick twist off the cap to inhale, th
room goes out in a blue staccato and you're hammered to th
finish by yourself in a storm and a roller coaster. Jamaica, yo
loved it, taking the ride alone and seeing the sights in som
neon hieroglyphic Persian while I held your hips and watche
the X's come up in your eyes. You wanted it every day, a
night, you wanted me to get you to the starting gate, pump yo
up for the real trip and keep the house from falling when th
floor moved: it was like fucking an electric zombie, a stiff-legge
gazelle shuddering in northern catatonia. Like dying in th
snowdrifts, Jamaica, moving on the floe of your body, white an
cold for miles. And I could wonder about shaking you until th
ice cracked and all the deep black poured out, textures
blacks: black of thick tar, black of satin, corduroy black, waxe
and petaled black of death masks, orchid black, black of cas
mere beds and the moonless impetigo night, cancer black an
black of inheritor insects, black of wet rope and burns and blac
and black and black I saw in your icy throat. I pulled you u
and shook you limp; Jamaica, you black doll, wobbling like
dead girl sewn of old socks. My hands were big enough to k
you. I threw you down and ran into the next room, cloude
coated with you; picked up that shoe box of delicates, amyl
trite in old Fabergé, Coty, Arpège bottles, and threw it again
the wall. The smell came up around us, liquefying air; for s
blank seconds I felt you under me again, twisting your bla
stripes. Raymond stood up to hit me with a nightstick some c
had given him for bennies, and Neinmann rotated his skele

ead to watch the fray; but it was when you came in, wild-
aired and wrapped in a sheet, that he rocked back and put up
is translucent stick-fingered hands. Even then he knew more
han I knew. Neinmann: now he knows all there is; the finish,
he big bang.

I might have finished with my hands at your throat. Where
ould we all be if I had; Obelisk still a destitute fortress and
Neinmann holding court a few thousand richer, rejoicing like a
ascist Munchkin in his broken-down Aryan heart: witch, witch,
he mean old witch, the wicked witch is dead. And Raymond,
where would he take his services; where would he find a seer, a
Mafioso Beatrice like yourself, a movie house scam the length
nd breadth of C Street? He watched me but you watched him.
Watched him and touched him, kept him in your apartment like
n accomplice court jester. And me Jamaica, I'd be in one of
everal Bolivias mourning your loss, bleeding my own menses
f regret at blowing the tracks of the only train that could push
he past a raunchy perfection; a save-my-soul rattle only the
evil searches out. I love you the way I love nightmare, secrets
oming up like smoke through a grid; the way I love mirrors
hattered but still whole, reflecting the foolish image in a
undred lit-up fragments. No one else could take me; pay my
ay with what your skin knows.

What about your heart. You dreamed it stopped and woke up
ith it pounding in your head, scraping across your insides like
he interminable drag of a foot toward some dead end. You
asped in your sleep then sat up swinging, like a man parting
ater for air. You wouldn't let me touch you. You put on your
othes, went to the living room and sat down in a chair op-
osite the couch where Raymond slept. He would feel you in

the room and wake up, sit across from you in his blankets, eye
trained on the wall past your face. You said he could help yo
because he wouldn't look, just kept his eyes open until yc
could sleep again. Then, when you were quiet, he picked u
your feet and held them in his hands. He put them in his la
and sat there, holding on. Finally he looked at the ceilin
stayed absolutely still. I know because I stood, prize son of m
prize mother, and watched him from the dark hallway. I sa
him turning on the axis of your legs. Once he bowed his fac
and put the clean ball of your foot to his forehead.

It was a ceremony I couldn't duplicate. I went back to ov
room and lay on the white bed. It started rotating slowly;
pressed my hands on the flat sheets; they were soft and worn
smelling of you. It was me in that room, in your bed, not hin
He could bring you around by not looking; you went away fro
me to let him; but it was me that saw you, and the games we
not really games. Who sees you now Jamaica, how many
them ever did. I got close, inside, in the whirling. Or mayl
you kept me out, crouched in your fetal hum, but I knew whe
you were and mapped a tonal geography no ear could nam
found you with a sonar plugged into that music of dark feedba
that shoves us. With you I'm blind as those flying rats wi
monkey faces whose ears are the one miraculous inversion th
keep them feeding themselves. Jamaica, I fed you whatever ye
wanted; sometimes I wouldn't stop.

Raymond was the icing on the cake. You kept the histo
vague; said you met him through friends who had grown
cracking meters together on North Broad Street. A few sm
deals later he was there and needed a place and didn't ask f
anything; you wanted someone alive in the rooms at night b
sides yourself and the roaches and the traffic sounds and t
street yells floating up past the windows. Maybe he was sor
kind of brother; he didn't talk too much, kept enough mon

around and knew how to get more. I moved in and you got the job at Obelisk; things picked up. I did the running; operations got smoother and bigger. Clockwork. I think about you out there walking on cement; the tick of your heels. Jamaica, whose clock was it?

You said Raymond was born to grow into that body, that hump like rhinoceros armor, his arms powerful and a little too short. He lifted weights every day and went to a welfare therapist twice a week, but he would end like a bug with its wings and lower thorax crushed, lurching in dwarfed circles on a sidewalk. He was arthritic; the disease crept up, would get worse and put him in a metal chair he could turn on with a switch.

He was gone most evenings, ate supper in a deli down the block and threw dice in a bar until late. We sat in our room with cold bottles of cheap Chablis and you told me he was usually in pain and got a lot of dope legally; that's how it started, he lucked into a doc who was a writing fool and then pushed those scripts on C Street until he was famous. Maybe too famous. I was convenient; I eased that particular pain.

Sometimes he gave you the creeps; he always knew it and disappeared for a few days. You touched my back, my chest, pulled my legs around you. We were alone and the rooms seemed bigger, stretched. We stayed naked in the daytime and made it, no amyl, on the kitchen floor. But by the time he came back we were ready for the sounds of him making coffee on the stove in the mornings, sitting in the corner place at the table, big-chested, Lancelot hair uncombed and so black the shine was purple, bent over acrostics and newspaper crosswords. It was tempting to see him as the handsome Jewish jock he would have been and he killed that temptation with a glance.

Maybe in those dreams you saw him crumpled up like a stunted spider, his back having taken him over. I told you I didn't know why he hung around for the slide, waited for that

slow engagement to suck him in. You mentioned certain contin-
ual numbers, said I would wait too, anyone would, wait forever,
because this was the only show in town.

Once we went walking by the junk stores and you bought a
boy's cap, an old woolen one with a snap brim and gold silk lin-
ing. Knickerbocker Superior Caps, said an oval inked label the
size of an egg, and it showed a wigged colonial with a ruffled
neck and a cane, ringing a bell. You tucked your hair inside it
and strolled, casual, by the mirror, making faces at me and pretending to twirl a walking stick. You looked for a long time at
the cigar holders and penknives in the glass cases, and finally I
bought you a miniature switchblade with a pearl handle.

I was born in the West Indies, you told me, And when we got
here my mother sold my ass right out from under me. She did it
with all the girls, five of us, until we got into our teens and left
home. She used to say our father left her because of us, and
now we could take care of things. No one ever really hurt us,
mostly playacting and harmless perv trips. I was the boy but she
never let me cut my braids; I wore them up, like this, in hats.

We were supposed to meet Raymond and Neinmann in a bar
closeby. We sat down and I asked what happened to that queen
of a mother. She aged fast, you said, Selling meat is hard work.
Her standard of living went down considerably after we all left
her. I hope she died in the gutter.

I asked if that tale about your father was a lie. Of course it
was, you said, We all had different fathers.

I looked down the street, watching for our cohorts. It made
me nervous to meet with them in public. Maybe they aren't
coming, I said, Maybe they're all enjoying that same crowded
gutter.

They'll be here, you said. Raymond always shows, and Neinmann will be around as long as we want him.

You bent your face to light a cigarette, hard jaw and downy
cheeks framed in the blousy cap. I forced your hand into the
ashtray and crushed the lit tobacco. You think you're moving us
around like little girls, I said, What about me, Jamaica? Think
I'll always show?

You looked me in the face and smiled. No, you won't show,
you told me, But you'll always be right where you need to be,
whether I want you there or not.

One show is like another. In the exercise yard the men walk
one of a dozen figure eights, trace their own dead tracks, wear a
subtle trench the width of a beagle's body. The far wall is covered with ivy and they head for that green color. On a quiet
windy day I stand close and the small stiff leaves are flapping
on the stone like hands that know one language. I work my
fingers through the tangled viny stems and the wall is mossy,
dumb, packed with cool soil in the cracks. Earthworms live in
the dirt, eating their tunnels. I see them loop in the leaves, fat
and pink, trail a lubricant smelling of ripe insides. Around their
middles there is a swollen band that veiled and bluish tint of
flushed skin. Press it and the worm rears a faceless end, delicate, smelling the air.

Inside is the clammy clank and slap of anywhere's jails. In a
few weeks I'm on my way to the pen, big-time gleam where I
learn a new career and swim awhile in the underbelly of that
metal whale. The whale eats what it's thrown and hums like a
city. During my wait the heat drops by every day, smooth heat
from the DA's office in expensive suits. No more street games;
it's big bucks, crooked rumba of the dodg'em politicians. They

tell me the whole story again: Neinmann in the burned-down Obelisk, a four-alarm fire in the A.M., and the old man crouched like a pile of spindled ash in the office by stacks of used reels. How like Raymond to fry Neinmann in his own thick oil, and do it so they can't prove arson. Or maybe Raymond didn't set it at all. And maybe it wasn't an intended deliverance I got handed the day the heat picked me up at that phone booth waiting for his call; maybe it wasn't them who were supposed to find me. Who was I waiting for? Jamaica, I like to think you had at least devised something quick for me; just a flash, an imprint before the black came up. Sometimes, lately, I like to think you devised nothing at all; that the sacred goons I imagine came down on you cleanly; that you're neck-deep in darkness yourself; then I turn off the light in my head and, like a fool, hope you'll be around to settle up with. Tomorrow I'll sing and sell you all; but, one way or another, you're all gone aren't you? and your names were only stories.

One, ten, twelve. Talk to me; go first. Games for two, trade sides and roll. Hold me; your back a broad olive blade that sharpens, slick with moisture, if we keep going. I could drink you up; lay down. I hold you like a baby, tell you I really love you, say words you like and then start dreaming on the downs, fading, passing through, big truck labeled with a bright red blur. You run the tub full of water before I'm too gone and walk me there in the fluid drunk of the pills. In the water you hold me under my arms, move the wet cloth on my skin and finally pull me over you, soapy and sleep-heavy. Water closes to our necks as you slide down under me; I keep my face on your skin to breathe and see your black body in silhouettes, a string of paper cutout dolls with joined hands who join hands around me.

umbling a thin white noise; and as they open their mouths I
ee their phosphorescent teeth glow a pale arpeggio. In the
vater obsidian beetles surface, doing their six-legged swims. I
ouch their hard shells and they crack, spill a silver mercury the
hickness of fish eggs. It clouds the water slowly, furling and
moky; in the smoke I see your hands moving water to reach
me. When you touch my flesh I slide out of it and wake up
standing, propped by your arms, your knee, the cold tile wall. I
eel the cloud still seeping from you and it dries on my hand,
cracking to a pile of charcoal numbers; dim serial of odd and
even, a catalog of fools.

At first, all the girls wore dresses. There was a checkered flag
of separation and the race was nothing on a board laid out with
paper money and plastic hotels for Park Place. There were
metal hoops to make points in and the balls sectioned off like
melons in orange and black. The rules were written down and
smeared in a fruity juice on all our faces.

The morning before I never saw you again, I opened my eyes
and your shorn hair was all over my naked front. You had cut it
to a jagged bowl around dawn, standing over me with scissors
and scattering the pieces.

The Powder
of the
Angels, and
I'm Yours

She remembered swerving, cocaine lane, snowy baby in her
veins. Like a white sock over her nose, smelling clean cotton in
dark halls of the seedy Plaza in Bogotá. Roaches glittered their
hard backs and the heavy Spanish flies buzz-droned, fucking in
midair. She met Hernando on the street in Cali, a few blocks
from the English school her parents had chosen to rehabilitate
her. He was high, strutting around with a red flowerpot on his
head and a green umbrella stuck in his hip pocket. 'Tis Our
Lady of the Stamens, he said to her in English. The rich Ameri-
cana. Daddy a government stoolie with a crazy daughter,
screaming since puberty about those voices under beds whose
instructions aren't clear. Paranoia, she told the psychiatrist,
sounds like an exotic liqueur. You drink it down hot and it

makes you shake. Hernando bowed and the clay pot smashed on stone.

She stole money for him. For his mouth biting her fingers as he slapped her hips and ground against her. Careening down midnight streets in her mother's long silk scarf, his body was a luminous black. They shot up in moss-walled bathrooms, blunt needle sinking like a nail's foot while jet-haired Catholic whores called from doorways. *Si, el polvo de los angeles, yo soy tuya. Tuya. Tuya.* She took photographs of his sinewy marked arms and sent them to her friends in the States. They ran coke and smack across the border in a flatbed truck with two borrowed babies and some goats tied in back. Their stench in the flat heat, Hernando dozing, his hands fisted. She felt them being devoured in the carnivorous satin flower of Colombia. They pulled off the road and squatted behind a chicken coop to fix. She saw he had done too much, his eyes glazed. The coke came up in her throat. She grabbed the needle from him and stuck it in a squawking rooster. Hernando hit her in the mouth, the maggoty chickens beating them with wings. A farmer came running out of the dirty house with a machete yelling *Monstruos, Monstruos*. She dragged Hernando to the truck, the farmer's bare feet chanting in the dust behind them. The dark babies looked up at her.

Rain in Washington for three weeks, first her uncle's house and now the sanitarium. She could see. Arlington Cemetery under gray pellets, rows of dumb stones. Embroidery. She pulled the thread in and out, working the plumed tail feathers. They asked her why she damned herself, they asked her why she didn't. All day Sunday the ministers came with their pamphlets. She liked to watch the priests in their feather-stitched robes. Blessing their vials of water, they touched fingers to the foreheads of the monstrous. *Domine domine*, they crooned, as each angel closed her eyes.

Stripper

When I was fifteen back in Charleston, my cousin Phoebe taught me to strip. She was older than my mother but she had some body. When I watched her she'd laugh, say That's all right Honey sex is sex. It don't matter if you do it with monkeys. Yeah she said, You're white an dewy an tickin like a time bomb an now's the time to learn. With that long blond hair you can't lose. An don't you paint your face till you have to, every daddy wants his daughter. That's what she said. The older dancers wear makeup an love the floor, touchin themselves. The men get scared an cluster round, smokin like paper on a slow fire. Once in Laramie I was in one of those spotted motels after a show an a man's shadow fell across the window. I could smell him past the shade, hopeless an cracklin like a whip. He scared me, like I had a brother who wasn't right found a bullwhip in the shed. He used to take it out some days and come back with such a look on his face. I don't wanna know what they know. I went into the bathroom an stood in the fluorescent light. Those toilets have a white strip across em that you have to rip off. I left it on an sat down. I brushed my hair an counted. Counted till he walked away kickin gravel in the parkin lot. Now I'm feelin his shadow fall across stages in Denver an Cheyenne. I close my eyes an dance faster, like I used to dance blind an happy in Pop's closet. His suits hangin faceless on the racks with their big woolly arms empty. I play five clubs a week, $150 first place. I dance three sets each against five other girls. We pick jukebox songs while the owner does his gig on the mike. Now Marlene's gonna slip ya into a little darkness Let's get her up there with a big hand. The big hands clap an I walk the bar all shaven an smooth, rhinestoned velvet on my crotch. Don't ever show em a curly hair Phoebe told me, Angels don't have no curly hair. That's what she said. Beggin, they're starin up my white legs. That jukebox is cookin an they feel their fingers in me. Honey you know it ain't fair what you do Oh tell me why love is a lie jus like a ball an chain. Yeah I'm a white leather dream in a cowboy hat, a ranger with fringed breasts. Baby stick em up Baby don't touch Baby I'm a star an you are dyin. Better find a soft blond god to take you down. I got you Baby I got you Let go.

El Paso

Dude

See I'd met this old dirt farmer in a bar the night before. Said he was selling his truck cheap and I could come down to La Rosa and pick it up. Said three hundred dollars and it didn't run too bad but I'd better buy it now. So I hitched down Sunday morning, mud churches on all three dirt streets ringing their black bells. I found him wringing a chicken's neck in the yard, did it quick and finished before he looked at me. Dark seamed face under a broad hat and the chicken head a little dangling thing hanging out his fist. I told him, said I'd come about the truck, did he still want—thinking we were both pretty drunk and he might have dreamed he had a truck, since it didn't look

like he had anything but a shanty house that leaned right into
dirt. He spat and turned for me to follow him, holding the
chicken now by a splayed leg that was bright orange in the rising heat. The nails on his hands were colored that same dull
shine as hen's claws.

Us walking in the dust yard past old tires and a rotten bed-
spring, mule tied to a pump by the chicken shed, and he stands
finally by this thing that's a red fifties Chevy with a built-on bed
shelved with chicken cages. Crosses and a blackened corn husk
doll hanging from the mirror, keys strung on a hair ribbon. I got
in and drove around the yard fast, chickens squawking and the
old cur dogs snapping at the wheels. The old man squatted
where he was, plucked the hen. Feathers flew and dropped as I
pulled up. I said the truck ran good and if he had the title I'd
pay him now and take it.

He motioned me inside a house somehow dark even in all
that light. Smell of wool shawls and vinegar. I stumble blind
into a table and voices, Spanish curses, stop and start. I look up
and Rita, she's standing there not three feet away, having
ripped the curtains off one window; she's screaming in her voice
that goes throaty and harsh, and the light pours in all over her.
Hot yellow gravy of light, her black eyes, and the red skirt
tight, blouse loose old lace ripped at the shoulder. I wanted to
roll my hand in her; I could feel her wet against my legs. The
old woman stands by the stove, side of her face shining, and
when she turns I see she's not crying but one eye weeps. Rita
walks past me steaming from her hands, the cheap plastic curtains clutched and dragging.

I watch the old man rummage in a drawer but feel her at the
end of the long room. Rita moving, bending over a small chair.
Old man counts the money and I turn to watch her. The light
rolling now, leaked into the dark, ripples the skin of the dark
and flies fly up in loose knots; low slow buzz in corners yellowed

and pulled out by the light that rolls across the surfaces of
things in yellow blocks. Dust in the light, and her body moving
down the long room pulls a white path like an animal leaving
water. She bends from the waist; under the cloth her thighs are
muscles, long curves. In the chair sits a baby whose head is too
big. His legs don't reach the floor; his skin is stretched tight and
pale like the light is under it. His hair is white and fine, swirled
on his man-sized head, and I know he is a child only by the way
he cradles a shoe to his face. Rocks the shoe slow in short arms.
Rita has her hands in his hair, her shoulders tensed and curved
to him. A sound catches in her throat and comes out low, folding into the yellow room. Thick juice of light circling, curling us
in. Child wheezing and rocking, rocking the shoe slow, his
mouth on it. It is her shoe and Rita croons, rocking with him,
pulling the shoe away.

Rita

I bought my mother those glasses so she wouldn't have to live
in the dark, spent a hundred dollars on an El Paso doctor so she
could see in the light without the eye burning. And she
wouldn't wear them. Would hide them and move like a bat in
the dark, the windows covered. The child in his chair with his
sounds, she singing her songs low in the dark, he weaving in his
chair. Me youngest of six, and at near fifty she gave birth to
him, his white skin and his head hanging like a heavy bloom on
the neck that couldn't move it. His eyes rolling back to see in
that head that must have been a field of snow inside. No father,
she said, he is what was in me. And the eye in her too, still
pouring from her slow. Bringing grain from the store on the
mule, she crossed against the light and a truck knocked her

down, the mule kicking her face. And so the eye weeps and
hurts in the daylight. Pounding meal on the wood table she
sings in the dark like she sang then, my five brothers building
cars in the yard, and me they called *brujita,* little witch.

At dusk the townspeople came to be healed. Paid her in corn
and cloth. Then the corn stacked by the door and tomatoes
hung to dry and sides of bacon, their white fat thick as my
waist. She in her white shawls and her almost black skin put her
hands in powders ground from roots. The villagers knelt, her
sound wheeling over them. Their eyes fluttered and their hands
unclenched, jerking as sounds came. *Muerte dios muerte
muerte.* They got up and bowed to the witch their children
won't touch. Castanets' slow dull clack followed them, their feet
going away in the dark yard. From the time I was a baby she
gave me a sharp stick and told me to draw them in the dirt to
keep their spirits from returning. She made her witching dolls
from husks; when I was older she gave me paints to draw their
faces. I made them: farmers' heads and goitered women already
old.

My father was gone long weeks to Las Vegas, Reno. Sometimes when he came back we moved to hotels in El Paso and
bought clothes in stores. Remember, she'd say, cracked voice
clacking on her teeth, you ain't no Spanish brats—You got
Gypsy blood and your daddy's Apache cheeks. I remember her
long fingers on my face. He didn't come back. The house was
her power and she wouldn't leave. The town still creeps to her
at dusk, women with shawls low over faces. The priest says it's
sacrilege, they heaping ashes by the door.

Already I was with men and she was big, her belly strained,
and the labor went two days. Women from the town wouldn't
help. She cut herself to let the child's head pass and the
women, hearing she had a devil, burned candles by their beds.
Later the old man came with his shriveled dolls, his silence,

d no name I ever heard her say. He built a chair on rollers
hen the child could sit and kept lanterns lit all night to make
e sounds soft.

Now the child's sounds are muffled and low except when I
nce. He knows me, holds out his hands for my shoes. My
other takes dried cactus from a wood box and grinds it, sprin-
es a powder on his hair. I make the signs and the castanets
arm in my fingers; we put the child's chair in the center of the
om and my feet on brushed boards start slow thud. The
um, her low voice quavering, my arms high, the clack silver
ack and the child's eyes focus, hold me fast, faster, me spin-
ing around him. He holds up his head, and under his skin I
e the pale blue veins. Faster, my feet pound floor, her voice
uder, and he whines a high clean whine that holds me spin-
ing. Ceiling twists, floor circles smaller, small. My hands over
im stop. Suddenly he sleeps, he sleeps and we lie, all of us, in
e hot dark house. Listen to him breathe.

The old man sells his truck, won't take my money. He sees
rls grind in city bars, knows how the money comes: my
oms, hotels, the avenue. The child's sounds are whispers
ow; he sleeps too long. At the white hospital, us black against
alls, they say the shunt in his head won't drain. He won't eat
nymore, drinks from bottles, watches me; why do I come here.
he hacks at the naked chicken on a board. Her face, the eye
rawn; I moving away through the yard. This dust on my legs
ellow as meal is burning, burning.

Dude

he walks out through dirt yard to the road. I run, touch her
rm. Her skin bare, dark walnut skin stained milky, and I stand,

my hand drenched in her skin, ask her, is she going back to
Paso. In the truck the land goes by us glaring as a lidless ey
sun a high glittering ring. Seeming to whirl in itself like ho
nets, it throws its heat on land laid out flat to the burning. W
glide horizontal on a strip of road. In the tiny room of the truc
I feel heavy in the rivery heat. Between us on the cracked seat
space gets small. Her satin skirt is faded in circles I could cru:
to my thumb. Under her heavy hair, her damp temples, I wa
to feel the shape of her skull. My hands are deaf. Eyes sto
with light she watches me try to see the road, her opaled ey
seeming to come out at me yet falling back in their deep oil th
scalds the side of my face.

I pull over, stop the truck, get out, lean against it. Up th
road a café, all night lights still on, runs a lit band of lette
around its roof: hamburgers, thick shakes, onion rings frie
gold. I walk up there and a woman with her hair dyed bra
swabs the counter with a rag. Her wide grin red, her front toot
gold, she lets me talk and counting change she fingers my palm

Ice cream packed hard melts slow on my hands as I'm wall
ing back. I see Rita hitching by the side of the road. I hand he
a cone, get in the truck and start the engine. She climbs i
Motor idling, sweet cold in our mouths, I pull her across th
seat and press my fingers hard at the base of her neck. M
breath comes out a ragged curve against her eyes.

Watching

He so in love with her it was something to see. Dude so caug
up and dedicated like a single eye to his own loving. How sh
touched it off. I suppose he was about to pack it in before h
saw her and thought there was still something to do. Walki

up the hill, touching him with her hip and walking, she moved; her hip was delicate and blue beside his thigh.

This was El Paso, 1965. She danced in topless bars, said really she was a painter but she needed supplies. Supplies she said are always hard to get, sometimes you just have to put out and get them and go off with them. It was plain he wanted to go off with her but in the summer in El Paso it's hard to move anywhere except down the street to the bars. I remember there was always dog puke on the sidewalks in El Paso. All those strays get the sweats around noon and bring up the garbage they ate in the back alleys of beanerys at dawn. Think about Texas and there's those skinny fanned ribs heaving.

Dude used to go down to Bimpy's nights and watch her dance. Bimpy was a greasy-kneed old faggot who liked him plenty and gave us free bourbon. She'd come over between songs and do a number with us, wringing with sweat so she'd wet the paper and we'd have to keep lighting it. She danced on this three-foot-square red stage, under two old ceiling fans that looked like little airplane propellers. She moved under their sleepy drone; always there was something about to break out. From our table in the corner I could smell the old roses smell of her. She was dark-haired and black-eyed though she swore she wasn't Spanish, medium-sized but small-boned with green apple breasts; then suddenly her twisted child-bearing hips that were somehow off-center and rolled gentle to the left when she walked, rolling slow up the hill past the plate glass liquor stores. Dancing, she'd throw her dusty scent past the two old spots Bimpy had and the cowboys threw bills on the stage. Dude hated the dancing; said she was frigid as hell afterward, like loving a wind-up doll except for her mouth and the curves it took on in the dark. She wouldn't even move with the lights on, he said.

After the show she'd stay and help Bimp sweep up and then

we'd walk out the door into the oily night. Everything wide awake and the fat yam-skinned women talking Spanish to their boyfriends, walking with their stemmed words and twined fingers past the blank-eyed 5 & 10's. We'd walk up the hill, they in front and me trailing behind. She talked in her Texas voice about nothing usually, it just being important there in the lit-up black to have her voice with its honeyed drawl and bitter edge; she walking slope slide up the hill, whisper of her nylons brushing and the Mexican boys shooting craps on the sidewalk. They ain't but thirteen, she'd say when they looked up at her heels clicking, Old enough. My daddy made a small fortune at craps. He used to call it dealin with the demon. She'd say that and slap Dude on the ass.

She'd boil those stark black Colombian beans on a stove in their flat and it'd heat up the kitchen so we'd have to sit out the window on the roof. By this time the town was near silent and steaming slow like a wet iron. Always drink hot coffee on hot nights, she'd say, Brings the sweat to the outside and lets you sleep. Dude dozed with his head in her lap and she'd turn to me, ask me, oils are on sale and could she borrow a few bucks till next week. You know, she'd say, twisting his hair in her fingers, Them stars are just holes in the sky after all. And while I'm sleeping in that hot bed everything I ever thought of having falls into em.

Finally I'd go to bed and hear them in the hall going back and forth to the bathroom, him usually drunk by then and tripping at the door. People up and down the hall behind doors yelled at him to shut up. Her arms reaching in the yellow blouse to grab the light string, her hips moving in their funny bumbling slow walk past my door, not quite touching his legs, and the mosquitoes louder than her quiet laughter: this was 4 A.M. in El Paso.

I saw him a couple of years later in Toledo, said he was into racing junk cars, said it was some kick. Said you're tearing

around and around under the lights in these things that are all
going to fly apart and pile up. Said he heard she was living
down in Austin with some dyke. Said cracking up those cars was
great, said he was making money and cracking them up was
some kick, it was really something.

Bimp

When I opened the place in '46 I didn't think no one could pull
nothin over on me again. I was in the war just like anyone else,
ain't no one gonna tell me I got any debt. I had enough tin food
and muddy boots and hair lice to last me. One goddamn big lie
is what it was, I figured that out. There ain't no losing or winning anywhere is what I figured out, ain't nobody gonna pitch
me into no fake contest again. I sailed into San Fran with a knee
like a corkscrew and the salt air made it ache like a bitch. I
came back home and opened the place and I figured I was
standing ground. Back then the Mexicans used to skunk around
at the alley door till I told em to beat it. I can see em now,
slinking off in their red shirts under that one streetlamp between the trash cans. My own grandmother was a Mex. She
smelled like a rotten cantaloupe and raved in Spanish about the
goddamn Church that did nothin but bury her endless brats and
the man that beat her. There ain't no losing or winning. These
black-eyed thieves and yellow Mex boys think I got something
they want, let em swagger in the front door so what. I could tell
em if they ask—no matter what they got they got more to get
and the thing don't end. Gaining like a squirrel on a wheel,
sure. When I saw them three kids I knew what the game was.
Her saying what I needed was a dancer, the dude pretty as a
rodeo star, and his sidekick one of them hunched-up watchers. I

said Listen, I got me a dancer, and she said Try me out. The
dude stood there grinding a butt into the floor in his high
heeled boots. I said Well I don't allow no dancers in here with
out escorts, gets plenty rough in here ya know, this ain't Philadelphia. She said she was from La Rosa, one of them dirt-eating
border towns, and I laughed, said You didn't get far didja. She
smiled, her mouth dark pink and those flashy Spanish teeth
strong as an animal's. The cowboy finally looked at me, said,
rolling the filter of his cigarette, We'll be here at nine. The
watcher stood there looking from face to face like he was judge
of the whole damn game and I said Suit yourselves.

Dude

Back then I was a carpenter like everyone. I quit school and
went down to Texas, air so thick and slow it's like swimming.
That flat-out heat comes after you and drinks you up; she'd been
there all her life. The steam in her; I lost what I was thinking in
rooms thick, full of us; her black hair in the sheets a wound
thread, thick black lines of drawings she kept hidden, her char-
coaled fingertips. She worked on the avenue, turned tricks in a
hotel room with a blue ceiling and one light bulb in a fringed
shade. I told her she had to stop it and she said well, she'd
dance but she wasn't carrying no slop to farmers in a beanery.
The difference is, she said, I say how I'm used.

By noon those days I was a walking fever, my hands cut and
sore from tarring feed store roofs, and since I first saw her I
come into the heat the place the heat like a bitch dog and lived
with it. When I got home it was late evening and she lay almost
naked on the roof. Past crooked streets the tracks ran off white,
cutting their light and crossing. Sluggish trains changed cars in

the hard-baked yard. Beside her on the shingled heat, I smelled her salt skin and she laughed, pulled my face to her throat. We rolled, hot shingles pressed to my back, and later the shower was cold. We drank iced whiskey in jelly glasses and she danced up the hall dripping, throwing water off her hair. In the stifled space, window at the end painted over and light through the cracked paint patterned on the floor, her back was beaded and swaying. Water backed up past the drain spilled cold past my feet onto the floor and in our rooms we wet the sheets, slept in their damp. Her hair looped in my hands dried slow: past us the trains whistled their open howls.

It was too hot to cook and we ate avocados, jalapeños, white cheese. City lights came on, blue and pink neon stood out cool and she leaning into the mirror painted her face for the bar. I forget all of it but her lacquered eyes. And she stepping off the curb in those high-heeled shoes, kids in Chevys grinning.

Sometimes she came back from Bimp's so late the light was coming up. Been with a john: she only did it she said when the money was too good to pass up. She'd come home with a bottle of brandy, get into bed with a pack of cards and we'd play poker to win till the sun was flat on the floor. Cards buckled finally and thrown against the wall, shades drawn, we lay there see, until we could talk. Her face in the white bed, her face by the window; light behind the shade as she stood there colored her face blurred and fading like a photograph. It's all right just come here.

Bimp

Like I said, I had another dancer. She was blond, from the East, up North I think. She had the look of someone didn't sweat much, just burned a coal inside. Ran off finally with some slick Mex to Panama. Could tell easy she was one to leave home over and over till her feet wore down to a root that just planted where she ran out of steam. The men liked that white hair and light eyes and those rhinestone shoes she wore. She had that hard crumpled look of a dame that's been around but don't know why. I knew she was thirty-five but I hired her anyway. Them white blonds is scarce down here.

I put em onstage together the first night and they set up a wheel the whole place was turning on, what with the smaller one and her seventeen-year-old's tits and them hips moving so you knew she'd been used since she was old enough to wiggle. Them border girls start with big brother in the alley, then towns full of female things dropping litters in the street. She moved with that clinched dark face, all of it a fist in her hips, and beside her the tall blond looked like a movie magazine none of em could touch. There was some kind of confusion, smelled like burning rubber. Spilt drinks and a goddamn brawl in the back at the card table. I got em offstage and turned up the lights and ordered everyone out of the place. Was just me picking up broken glass and the girls leaning by the bar and the two men dealing a hand at the corner table like nothing happened. The girls were dressed, the blond fooling with her necklace, talking low. Her blue eyes drinking that Spanish mouth she say soft, Hey Honey, how long you figure on dancing with that swayback of yours and that funny hip—damn, can you get this thing fastened—no, here—Lemme put it on and you can maybe pinch it with your teeth—She leans over the Spanish, her red lips apart like she's still talking, beer tipped in her hand and dripping all over their stockings. And the smaller one, black hair to her waist, hands midway in the air, stands there like a stone saying over and over, I can't fix it, I can't fix it.

After that I had em alternate nights and a week later the

blond split. The cowboy and his sidekick was in here nights
with the Spanish, the two of em diddling with cards and race
forms in the corner. Figure it's been ten years ago. Gave me a
few good tips and then same as now—when I hit at the track I
blow it all same night, ain't nobody gonna tell me I won nothin.

The Blond

Rita. She left the avenue, the hotel, smell of urine and spent
sex in the halls. We traded johns and other things; me by her
door in blue light, cognac in my hand and my robe open. I
asked her low, A toast to the hungry jokers? mouth on my
raised glass and she let me in . . .

She let on like we never knew each other, but them hot
nights I told her stories. Like how it was when I was seventeen
like her. Ginette Hatcher was my name then, in Maine all the
gray years. She born and died in Maine, she dying there still I
guess. I took the name the first truck driver gave me, called me
Babe and I answered to it ever since. I left my husband that I
only saw in the dark after the boats came in or before they went
out, that man always cold and fish slime on his hands. I left soon
as the baby was born, thinking the best anyone could tell the
kid was that Mama took off. There something out there besides
that gray wet, that heavy roll. My cousins and uncles was all
lobstermen ever since I can remember. My dad too, but he
died when I was so young all he is to me is a furred chest and
smell of oiled rope. He died of lobster is what Mom said, and
she killed hundreds of them. Scratch-clink of those claws against
the boiling pot was a woman sound, a metallic scratch round as
rings.

Wind and rock and weeds on the beach a gray stink, no color

cold; I kept fish eyes in bottles and sold them all summer to the tourists, to the queers and dandies and the painted old things with poodles. Once an old woman with money asked me to come to her hotel and read the Bible to her. She opened it and I started in. After a while I looked up and she was staring out the window like a sleepwalker, her old hat in her lap. She said what a blessed child I was to come to womanhood here by the sea, so far from heat and corruption. I said Yes Ma'am. The fire comes from the feet, she said, from the walkers and the black hair. She didn't see me anymore. I grabbed my sweater and ran home across the hotel beach, the big umbrellas blind and rolling on their sides. I found twenty dollars folded in my pocket and I bought me some red patent leather spike heels. I hid them in my room and only put them on at night and I was the walker walking and the dancer dancing in my fiery feet, and holes in the floor where I burned through.

Tires on the big trucks burn. You smell them in the cab, smell the motor boiling; my suitcase wedged between my knees and the truckers touching my dress. I lived everywhere and been to Mexico. I danced mostly, waited tables, worked in a library once and couldn't feel my feet for the shiny floor. Down in Texas any man on the street would buy me supper. By the time I got to Bimp's those nights I was already loaded. Blur, dark oiled skins past the lights, ice in glasses. Cold melts in a circle, hot whiskey, hot Texas. And Rita shows up, so smooth and so hot; eyes like black glass, sunk in, burned young. On-stage she scared me, made that cold ocean roll in my head . . . then the lights were on, jeers from the floor, and that little pimp pushing us stumbling into the dressing room. Where I lean against the wall and watch her shaking by the sink, cold water on her wrists, and we look at each other. They say the world ends in fire and ice; I say it's already over. That hot pave-

ment burns you straight through; that's why I did it, kept
moving—no slow cooking and my claws raking walls. These
streets, raunchy brass, my feet on fire burns up that dead ice.

I split way south with a rich dude. Red birds and black-eyed
men. Been some since then. I'm doing OK, I got it made, and
the cold don't come so much now.

Rita

I lived with Dude those months in two rooms, rickety bed on
blocks and past the windows the roof steamed between shingles. Long afternoons I cut the thin tar bubbles with my nails,
oils warm on the paper, and the tubes heated till their lettering
came off in my hands. I drew the trains: red gashes and the
tracks black rips underneath. His hands felt furred with dust.
When he was roofing, tar smudged the lines and crosses in his
palms, left the whorls of his fingers and their black smell on my
hips. Some days we stayed in bed, kept the fans turning, buzzing; we had cold wine and coarse brown bread. At night the
bars were crowded with drunks, some of them sick in the heat.
Dancing, I didn't watch them; I saw the flat brushed land outside the house in La Rosa, looking tawny-colored from the
shaded rooms, but out there, walking, you felt hard hot sand
and the color spreads into a wasted brown.

I think of what happened and it happens each time the same
way. When I go back they are padding the cart with skins. Inside in his bed the child's face is drawn and blue. He breathes
faint strangled bleats and my mother waits, sewing pelts to wrap
him. At dark she feels his throat and says there's no breath; we
leave with the cart. In the skins his face is white and his light

hair long as a girl's. The hitched mule swings its head, flare
nostrils at the fresh smell and moves skittish toward the hills
The old man bends in brimmed hat, shuffles to low chant, an
she walks behind, scatters fine powder on the ground. Car
rocking slow and the child's face in my lap is sunken, lids o
rolled eyes tight closed. All night we keep moving on the slope
land. Sand rolls its barren striped bars; the sky is inked an
slashed in the foothills where we stop, take bundled wood from
the cart, tie it with cords. She knots leather in the dark and th
old man's voice is hoarse. At dawn she piles brush and th
corded wood; we lift the child, straining, jangling the bracelet
on his arms. She lights dried skins wrapped on a stick, touche
him, and he starts to burn. The wood catches and through th
fire I think I see his face move. It moves again and I throw he
back, digging, clawing at the hot wood under him. They watc
me try to reach him, now he is all fire. Running around th
stench I fall and their old faces over me say I only dreamed it.
smell the skins and his flesh, the incense burning under him.

Mule leading then down the ravine to where the ligh
stretches out on land like a smooth film of egg. I stumble and
touch the animal's hide, feel ribs under stiff mousy hair. The ol
man walks ahead, his back a leathered board under cloth. She
stays there by the smell until it is finished; quiet, she waits to
take the bones.

Hours walking, sun high and the road a sudden empty strip
The old man waits for me, then turns in the glare and tells me
again that I dreamed it. I see his knife and serape on his waist,
know he's not going back for her. I won't go back to her either.
Smoke in my mouth, I smell the wheeling birds and the tigh
white face behind the bristled fire. Old man walking away on
the road with his mule and there are trucks, horns, voices, Baby
wanna ride?

*   *   *

Dude

remember the rains had started, blown in off the Gulf. She'd
been to La Rosa. Always when she came back she was this
hunted dog, stringy and gutted and ready to gnaw its own foot.
came in and she was walking circles in the room, rubbing her
hands. I saw her fingers were torn, bruised purple under the
nails. The rolled drawings were torn and smoldering on the
floor. I moved to stomp them out and heard her moan, turned,
saw matches in her hands; she striking and tossing them in the
air where they'd flare and fall smoking. I grabbed her arms and
everything was breaking, chairs cracking on the floor and the
light bulb splintering. I saw her hair on fire under my hand and
I rolled her onto the bed. All the time she moaned long and low
like I wasn't there except that this thing was on top of her. Her
eyes were calm and her burned hair broke in my hand. I pulled
her down and heard my breath coming high and watered like a
woman's; she fell and lay there, her lips moving. She drooled
and the spit flecked red where her teeth had cut. I stood over
her and yelled for her to see me. Her eyes rolling past me
pulled my hands to her clothes and the cloth ripped. I slapped
her, kept slapping her and my hands were fists. I looked up and
he's watching us—always goddamn watching us—then he is
talking quietly and pulling her from under me.

Watching

He was ramming his fists into the floor beside her head but he
thought he was hitting her and asked me later had he killed her.

The floor was splintered, fine wood in his hands, and she und
him stared glazed at the ceiling. Her mumbled Spanish mixe
in the room with the sulfur smell of something burned. When
pulled her from under him I saw her hair was burned ragge
and her shirt seared in the back. I took it off and wrapped her
blankets; she was shivering. There was broken glass and he
fingers were bloodied somehow. She kept talking to nothing
tossing her head from side to side, hands clinched in my hair s
tight that when I lay her down I can't move from her. Have
bend over her, my face close though she doesn't see me; I touc
her lips, the cuts scabbing and her teeth flecked with the du
dried blood. I smell her breath coming shallow and fast, say he
name over and over until she hears me. Almost focusing sh
slides her hands slow from my hair down my face to her breast
holding them.

Late that night, Dude sits by the window. Rain spills in; h
watches the smoky trains jerk in the yard, moisture on warm
soot a fine dust in the air. He blinks like he's slapped when h
hears her clutch her throat and turn in her sleep. I talk, Dud
smells her on his split knuckles, and the streaked curtains mov
all night.

Toward morning he paced the room, circling from door t
window. Hands held delicate, he looked at me. His eyes I thin
were gray and heavy-lashed; the lid of the right one droope
and softened that side of his face. Finally he turned and left; h
pointed boots tapped a faint click on the stairs each step down

She woke up in twisted blankets and raised her fingers to he
face. We ate the bread slow, her mouth bleeding a little. I'r
seeing her in summer by the stove in their room, sweat cloud
ing her hair and her lips pursed with cheap wine; she smoothin
her cotton skirt and throwing back her hair to bend over th
burner with a cigarette, frowning as the blue flame jets up fast
On the street under my window she is walking early in the day

tight black skirt ripped in the slit that moves on her leg. Looking back she sees me watching and buys carnations from the blind man on the corner, walks back, tosses them up to me. She laughs and the flowers falling all around her are pale, their long stems tangling. The street is shaded in buildings and her face turned up to me is lost in black hair. She is small and she is washed in grilled shadow.

Fingers too swollen to button her shirt, she asked me would I get her something to soak them in. At the drugstore buying antiseptic and gauze I felt her standing shakily by the couch, touching her mouth with her purple fingers. Walking back fast I knew she was gone, took almost nothing. The ashed drawings were swept up and thrown probably from the window. He left for good soon after, thirty pounds of Mexican grass stashed in the truck for a connection in Detroit. I went far north as I could get, snow that winter in Ottawa a constant slow sift that cooled and cleaned a dirt heat I kept feeling for months; having nothing of her but a sketch I'd taken from where she hid them: a picture of trains dark slashed on tracks, and behind them the sky opens up like a hole.

Under the
Boardwalk

Her name is Joyce Casto and she rides our school bus. The Castos all look alike. Skinny, freckled, straw-haired. Joyce's is the color of broom sage, dried out by some heat in her head. She walks the halls of the junior high with a clipboard of ruffled papers, transistor radio beating in her hand.

Daddy is a fire-and-brimstone preacher at a church out the dirt road. Music is the work of a devil that licks at her legs. She stands, radio pressed to her face, lips working. Undah the boardwalk, down by the sea ee ee ye eh eh, Ona blanket with my baybeh's where I'll be.

She walks into class fumbling to turn it off. Stays close to the wall and watches the cement floor. She never talks to the country kids. The town kids never talk to her. The gym teacher

finds out she is pregnant. Yes, she confesses, It was my brothe
He's went off to the mills.

She disappears from school but comes back a month late
having had it in a bloody way. She rolled up a horse blanket ar
walked to the field. Daddy thundering I won't lay eyes on yor
sin and big brother in Youngstown, holding a thing that bur
orange fire. She rolls, yelping, dogs come close and sniff. Th
circle. The sky circles. Points of light up there that sting. F
nally she sees they are stars. Washing herself in the creek sl
remembers the scythe against the grass, its whispering rip.

Next morning she sits in the house alone while the othe
shout and sweat at a revival in Clinger's Field. The dogs con
in with pieces in their mouths. She stands in the kitchen sha
ing while the Drifters do some easy moanin.

Sweethearts

We went to the movies every Friday and Sunday. On Friday nights the Colonial filled with an oily fragrance of teen-agers while we hid in the back row of the balcony. An aura of light from the projection booth curved across our shoulders, round under cotton sweaters. Sacred grunts rose in black corners. The screen was far away and spilling color—big men sweating on their horses and women with powdered breasts floating under satin. Near the end the film smelled hot and twisted as boys shuddered and girls sank down in their seats. We ran to the lobby before the lights came up to stand by the big ash can and watch them walk slowly downstairs. Mouths swollen and ripe, they drifted down like a sigh of steam. The boys held their arms tense and shuffled from one foot to the other while the girls sniffed and combed their hair in the big mirror. Outside the neon lights on Main Street flashed stripes across asphalt in the rain. They tossed their heads and shivered like ponies.

On Sunday afternoons the theater was deserted, a church that smelled of something frying. Mrs. Causton stood at the door to tear tickets with her fat buttered fingers. During the movie she stood watching the traffic light change in the empty street, pushing her glasses up over her nose and squeezing a damp Kleenex. Mr. Penny was her skinny yellow father. He stood by the office door with his big push broom, smoking cigarettes and coughing.

Walking down the slanted floor to our seats we heard the swish of her thighs behind the candy counter and our shoes sliding on the worn carpet. The heavy velvet curtain moved its folds. We waited, and a cavernous dark pressed close around us, its breath pulling at our faces.

After the last blast of sound it was Sunday afternoon, and Mr. Penny stood jingling his keys by the office door while we asked to use the phone. Before he turned the key he bent over and pulled us close with his bony arms. Stained fingers kneading our chests, he wrapped us in old tobacco and called us his little girls. I felt his wrinkled heart wheeze like a dog on a leash. Sweethearts, he whispered.

1934

In 1934 I was seven years old. Bellington, Virginia, was a Depression town. My mother was twenty-eight, my father fifty, my grandmother sixty-two. We lived in a big falling house in the center of town; but in those days, forty years ago, even town people had some land, barns in back. We had cows, some chickens. If it weren't for them we'd have starved because my father was crazy.

All morning my grandmother, Jocasta Andora, churned butter on the porch. I believed she had a rat in the tall urn. Determined, scowling, she beat it to death every day. Nonstop, blunt tick of a clock. She kept her white hair twisted in braids and wore a man's wire glasses with bent frames. She got up at five with Lacey, my mother, and started as soon as the cows were milked: pounding, pounding, pounding. She kept on until eight when we left in the cart and she walked over the hill to give blind Aunt Jenny her insulin shot. Until then I had to stand beside her while she molded the pale yellow bricks. I had to run them to the icehouse while she flicked at my heels with a broom.

"Run! Run! Before the mold smears! You'll be your father's daughter yet . . ."

Lacey and I delivered milk and butter and eggs in a cart. Some mornings our neighbor Johannes helped us load up. Tall and blond, Swedish, he said our names in a singsong. He had the high, broad forehead of a child, and a wife who seldom spoke. As we rattled away in the cart he raised an arm and held it, motionless, until we were out of sight. Lacey never turned.

She had a red account book the size of my palm. I held it in my lap, read names and orders over clinks and grumbles of the cart. Lacey's chestnut hair strayed in her eyes. She had one muslin dress she saved to deliver orders; said she refused to look poor in the shops. Storekeepers on Main Street stopped us, asked after J.T. She'd say he was improving thank you. They shook their heads, he was a compatriot who'd deserted them. Besides, everyone in town knew he was only getting worse. Weekly, he'd start downtown in the middle of the street, shirtless, in his nightcap. He wouldn't budge for horses or autos. Just kept striding, shaking back his long hair, probably to the bank to demand his money. Of which there'd been none for five years.

"Take off your pants, J.T.!" Jocasta snarled it from the kitchen, sometimes she yelled it from the window. "If you take off your pants, they'll make her put you away!"

Lacey rushed to the door after him.

"No, Lacey," sighed Jocasta. "Let the child."

So I was sent.

"Pop, the Gypsies are at the house."

"Eh, what? What?"

"The Gypsies, Pop, they're ready to pay."

He'd mumble about settling accounts, let me take his hand, lead him to the wooden sidewalk. We'd go home.

Some days he appeared to be lucid, though he never acknowledged he was poor. Every morning after breakfast he went to his office on the top floor, dressed in his old spats and a bow tie. He had all his account books up there, boxes of them, and he notated every page. He'd been through them all several times; drawing minute red lines and arrows through the words, and quotes from Shakespeare. He imagined I was a boy, his partner in the business. I had one of his cigars I'd chew and pretend to smoke. He'd light it for me, leaning forward, rippling his thick brows, intent on his hand and a cupped flame which wasn't there. His close breath smelled of soap and tobacco. Fine black hair thickened at his wrists. He wore gold cuff links on his shabby shirts.

We could see the whole town from our third-floor windows: Main Street curving down under oaks to where the river curled in a turn, gas-lit globes on the bridge, the junkman on his bicycle. Our tall windows were set thickly in walnut; dark stain dried and flaking to let the wood show naked. Dust floated in the shafted light. J.T.'s lips were the dark pink of sexual flush. He had begun to age with a strength and promise of frailty, flesh across his broad-boned face gone a faint rose in the blue shadow of his beard. He called me Frank instead of Francine.

"Now, Frank. Mr. Southern will arrive here approximately noon. I want you to go down by the river and oversee the cutting. I'll keep him busy here until the wood is stacked."

Southern was a big New England account he'd lost before the mill dissolved. J.T. was once a rich man, owned the biggest lumber operation in the state. He had a whole town of look-alike workers' shacks down by the river in Hampton, ten miles from town. Now they were empty, all the blind cracked glass broken out. My mother eloped with him when he had four grown kids older than she, the finest house in Bellington (historical societies offered to buy us out every year), and lumber operations in six towns. When they came into the station on the train after the wedding trip, his workers lined the tracks and cheered.

"Tail chaser," Jocasta sneered at him. "Out chasing tail every spare minute. No wonder you lost everything. Credit to Gypsies!" she snorted.

"Mother," said Lacey. "What's done is done."

"Yes, and it's done to us. You ought to put him away. He's nothing but a cross."

She and J.T. had fights. Sometimes he'd sneak up and pretend to pick lice off her clothes. I liked that. He would nip at her hair with his fingers until her combs fell out, Jocasta's silver hair falling down all around her. She screamed in fury. Her erotic hair was dangerous; loosened only late at night in her room, thick, blue-silver halfway to her knees. She stayed alone, combing, behind the locked door. Brushing, she watched her circular mirror; sang her high wheedling hum that floated up to my third-floor bed. Across the hall in his room my father listened too. He seemed never to sleep; all night his dim light burned. I saw Jocasta's hair hanging to the rungs of her chair. Yes, I believed I saw it. I wanted to touch her hair. I wanted to wrap myself up in her secretive hair. Ten years later when Jocasta died, I helped Lacey comb out the long and menacing hair. It felt like the mane of a horse.

J.T. used his full charmed strength against Jocasta. She threw every pot in the kitchen at him. Occasionally he threw them back. Lacey and I stood and watched, she yelling "Mother! Not the breakables!" Jocasta picked up something to throw every time he came near her. When she churned, he came up behind her. She'd grab one of the heavy butter molds.

"J.T., you'd look well if I hit you between the eyes with this." She stood facing him, brandishing the mold and holding to her glasses with one hand.

Lacey's father, Jocasta's husband, Herbert, owned a hotel where J.T. used to stay the night on business trips. The first time Lacey saw J.T. she was sixteen, night clerk at the check-in desk. J.T. was thirty-eight, a powerful full-chested man with jet-black hair, a boutonniere and gold-tipped cane. He gave Lacey a diamond wrapped in a handkerchief and said she would marry him. For a year Jocasta kept it from happening, then Herbert died of cirrhosis and Lacey eloped. Jocasta raved on about cursed women and bad choice.

"God knows your father was a wretch. You should have done a sight better in picking one for this child."

Lacey had brown eyes of a depth and shine that always looked welled with tears. "Mother," she said, "You know they were both so charming and fine."

"And what does charm get you? A lunatic or a drunkard. If you'd had a decent father yourself you'd never have tried to marry one, an old man."

"Mother, he wasn't old. He's still not old."

"To a girl of sixteen a man near forty is old, or should be. I tried to tell you that too, a dog that'll carry a bone will bring one. You were a child. He was six years younger than your own father."

"That's just because you robbed the cradle."

"It's best for a woman to marry a younger man. Women outlast men, we're both proof. They don't have our stamina. Marry a young one and you can count on him to bury you."

"Mother, Herbert died long before you will."

"Only because he drank." She sniffed and lifted her chin.

Jocasta kept a locked iron box under her bed. She kept all the baubles J.T. had lavished on Lacey during their courtship. She maintained that those jewels were our security. She even bought back necklaces and watches J.T. had given his mistresses. Wrote letters all over the state offering to buy or trade for them. Then she wrapped them in clean rags and put them in the box. Kept her door locked, carried a long skeleton key on a thin gold chain fastened to her belt.

Jocasta was obsessed with money. All her life she'd barely held on to it, managing the hotel while Herbert drank away the profits. Over and over, she tried to talk Lacey into selling J.T.'s old car, a 1928 Ford locked in the garage. J.T. had it polished until light glanced off like a knife, but he kept driving it top speed down the sidewalks and the town council got out an injunction. Sometimes he walked out at night, looked in the round garage window at the car shining in old smells and dark.

"That car sits out there for six years while we struggle to feed ourselves. That money could roof the barn and buy us another cow. Francine's getting old enough to milk, she can assume her share of the load—"

"Assume her share? She's seven years old and she's seen to J.T. this past year, something you nor I can manage."

"Well, I mean with the economy of the household. If we don't sell that car soon, there won't be a soul left in town with money to buy it."

"There isn't a soul now."

"Yes there is. John Simpson asked me about the car yester-day. I was down at the bank and—"

"Simpson! Just the one J.T. would hate to have it. That man profits on trouble, he's a sniveling crook. I still think there was something shady about the Trust."

The Trust was a fairy tale of which I often heard. When I was born, my father set up a trust to be awarded me when I was ten. Simpson said that when J.T. got so deep in debt that the mill was at stake, he revoked the trust to cover deficits. He lost the mill anyway. Simpson had papers J.T. had supposedly signed, but Lacey thought he'd signed them himself and em-bezzled the money, covered it somehow with his shifty lawyer mind. She called in other lawyers.

"Gentlemen," Simpson told them. "A shame J.T., a man of stature surely, lost his reason, but the facts speak for them-selves. Fifty thousand dollars for a child of ten? Isn't that in it-self a little illogical? I tended J.T.'s business as long as possible. We were friends for years, but you can't save a man who's drowning."

Lacey told how he sat there in his big chair looking sorrowful. Simpson weighed three hundred pounds. His limpid blue eyes slanted almost Asian at the corners; he moved his big body with a feline ease. His lips had a swollen look. He pursed them, touched my neck when I delivered milk on Main Street. He stroked me, lightly, with his manicured hand. Lacey looked stiffly away. Once he leaned into the cart, got close to her over my head and talked to her low and breathy.

"You needn't be so high and mighty," he said. "I could do things for you in this town."

I kicked him hard in the center of his fleshy chest. My boot left a black print that pointed at his throat as he cursed and we drove off. "Damn you! She's the seed of her father! They'll both end in the asylum! To hell with you!"

Bottles bounced and clinked in the cart. I asked if it was true I'd go crazy.

"Of course not. You're like the women in the family, sound as a dollar."

"But Grandmother says I'm like him."

"Don't pay mind to that. She's just jealous because she didn't love her father like you love yours."

"Why not?"

"Because he was an invalid who smelled of camphor and never got out of bed. He used to make her tie her wrist to the arm of her chair and do needlepoint while he took his naps. He lectured her on demons. He was an evil old man."

"Lacey," I said. "I don't know if I love my father. He doesn't even know I'm a girl. Sometimes I hate him."

"I know, Francie, sometimes I do too."

My father's secrets chased us all. At fifty he was still a big man with powerful arms. His grayed hair curled thick and long over his collar before he'd let Lacey cut it. Every few weeks he'd get to drinking. Be docile, childish, speak to Lacey as though she were his mother. She'd tie a bib around his neck, sit him down, shave him and cut his hair.

After he was spruced up he'd grow thoughtful. Walk slowly upstairs in his bare feet, shower, put on aftershave and his green silk vest. He'd put on his straw boater, still almost new because he seldom wore it, and walk to the drugstore after candy.

"Oh, Lord," groaned Jocasta as he came down the steps.

Lacey hushed her, said, "Francie, go after him."

And I'd walk him downtown. "Frank, my boy," he'd say, and put his arm around me. He'd tip his hat to all the women. He was a very handsome man, my father. He'd fairly swagger with happiness, and everyone on the street spoke to him. They'd nod and shake hands eagerly, the men anxious to talk. At the dry goods store, he'd ask Mrs. Carvey about her children.

"How's Bill doing in the sand lots? That boy has a genuine pitcher's arm, Miranda, he should have training, it's a fact."

Bill had grown and gone before my father married my mother, but Mrs. Carvey went on just like he was nine years old. Her husband was dead; she was lonely. She'd get feeling so good she'd pile me up with remnants to take home. That was how Lacey made my clothes.

Then we'd go down to Farmer's Drug. Cy gave J.T. a box of candy and put it on the imaginary bill. Cy loved J.T. He even slipped Lacey sleeping powders to sedate him in the bad times. J.T. had staked Cy in pharmacy school and again when he started his store. Cy gave me sodas so J.T. would stay and talk to him. Pop always thought it was Sunday when he was in the drugstore and he'd ask for a paper.

"Nope, not in yet this morning, J.T. Come back this afternoon."

"Well, I'll do that, Cy."

They'd shake hands and clap each other's shoulders. Once Cy started tearing up.

"Now, boy, none of that," said J.T. "Times are getting better, you'll see. And if you have trouble with the store, you know I'm right here with whatever you need."

Out front we'd sit down to discuss the stock market with the men.

"I tell you, boys, the market won't go down. It may waver, but it stands firm."

Of course everyone but he was painfully aware the market had crashed in '29, but they sat discussing the possibility very seriously. They took sides, argued loudly. J.T. and his supporters usually won. They all sat believing in futures.

Finally J.T. got up and stretched, winked, said someone waited for him. He'd whistle all the way home and seem to forget me. He knew the way, he owned the street, I walked behind him. He'd begin to smooth his now-cropped hair and clear his throat.

We could smell our kitchen from down the block. Butter-fried chicken, new potatoes, Jocasta's buttermilk biscuits. Flowers on the swept porch. J.T. made his entrance, swept off his hat grandly, flourished the box. When he spoke to Lacey, white in her muslin dress, J.T. stuttered; something tugged in his brain but he got past it. He took Lacey's hand and folded it to his mouth.

Through dinner she glanced at him, small penetrating glances, as he argued quietly to Jocasta about Galsworthy, whose collected green-bound volumes he read alone in his room at night. Lacey watched them both, twisting her dress beneath the table.

I cleared the plates and she turned on the phonograph, handled heavy waxen records until the old waltzes tinkled out at the right speed. J.T.'s eyes were bright; he whirled her around the room while Jocasta sat downcast. Finally they'd go upstairs as soon as it was decently dark, Lacey's hair falling from the dancing. The record finished and kept scratching, needle bouncing back and forth.

The wind blew the curtains in billowed forms. The glories closed on their vines. We could hear the old brass bed upstairs

beginning, rocking very gently. Sometimes Jocasta turned the
music on again. Sometimes we just sat, looking at each other,
while the rocking went on; small swooning cries, sharp jabs of
the bed against the wall.

During a summer storm, lightning struck the barn. Out the
back window a rosy flame burned its petaled center, a cauli-
flower of fire and smoke. We ran outside, the neighbors came,
we passed buckets for twenty minutes. J.T. supervised in his
pajamas, lined up the men and women, pumped water at the
trough. Stark-faced in the jumping light, his voice booming, he
yelled directions.

"Get the lions and tigers out!" he kept shouting. "Don't let
the big cats burn!"

But the hay caught, the rain slacked. Everything burned except a few chickens and one cow Lacey saved at the risk of her
skin.

At the end of it, she stood transfixed by the trough as all the
people dispersed. Our neighbor Johannes went to her in the
dark and took hold of her. He held her and rubbed her back.
"There now, there." She clung to him, grabbed one of his hands
behind her and held it. His ashed face nearly shone with some
power. He said to come, let him give her some coffee and
whiskey. But she said no, she only wanted to stand here for a
while. Johannes touched her face, stroked her hair. Picked me
up and carried me to his house, and his wife gave me a bath.

Johannes's wife was a wispy woman considerably older than
he. She was actually his cousin once removed. They had left
Sweden together, she thirty-one and he seventeen, both un-
married virgins. It was a long hard trip, and lonely. When they
got to New York he married her. She thought she carried a

child but she was wrong. Johannes's wife was barren; she had female problems. Some weeks she stayed in bed.

But that night she bathed me. She smelled of lavender. She lit the bathroom with candles, she sprinkled potpourri and spearmint in the steaming water. She made it bubble with bath salts. Rubbed me with a sponge as big as two hands and I was drunk with flowers. All the time she sang and muttered in her broken English, "Fire no good, poor fire."

She lifted me out of the tub, swaddled me in towels and carried me, though she was frail, into a room where she kept her dolls from Sweden. More lamps, she lit them all, on the floor and the windowsills. Tall globes threw tangled shadows about the walls. Shadows of the dolls' limbs loomed huge across the floor. Dolls, twenty or thirty, in big gossamer hats or bonnets with feathered parakeets, long tulle dresses, buttoned shoes. Their rose faces were perfect in a shadow of curled lashes. They posed sitting, standing, walking, running, holding dishes, bouquets, smaller dolls. One wore roller skates, another walked a stuffed Scottish terrier on a leash. That night was my first hallucination. The dolls began moving around the room, rolling hoops with sticks and talking in their whispery, breathless voices. Johannes's wife was talking too. Her Swedish got faster and faster. She went walking around with the dolls, their glass eyes glazed. They kicked their feet out straight in front. I saw it, the goose-stepping dolls, naked and seven in that room.

"Gerta!" Johannes's voice. He switched on the electric light. Spoke to her with harsh resignation and came to me on the rotating carpet. He pressed my face to his blond beard. The dolls' faces still moved, secretly.

Lacey's face was drawn and tight. She came to get me at Johannes's house the next morning, my best white dress folded on her arm. She stood in the doorway, her hair pulled back severely and her muslin dress freshly ironed.

"Francie," she said. "We're going to the bank."

We turned, walking. Wet grass spattered her stockings. At the garage she stopped, opened the old locks and let the creaking doors swing wide. The earthen floor rose its buried scent around our heads. When Lacey closed us inside, a powdered light sifted through the dirty window. I saw the board walls grown with chartreuse moss, old sleigh bells hung on leather straps, and something massive glinting in the middle of the room. It seemed to palpitate and breathe, then I saw the movement was only a casting of light on its hard black sides. Chrome and patent black. My eyes grew accustomed to shadows and the car emerged glimmering its saucered headlights. Smells of wax and leather mingled in the dark. Lacey knelt and stripped me. She fastened the dress, nails of her cool fingers scratching my skin. She stood then and walked around the car, touching it with one extended finger.

In the bank we waited, Lacey staring straight ahead. Simpson's secretary, Bedelia, sucked her pencil. Two bright red spots in her cheeks jumped out. She watched Lacey and hated her. Bedelia wore long chains of fake pearls like the women in New York City, but in truth Simpson had found her not twenty miles from town when he foreclosed the mortgage on her father's gritty farm. Bedelia kept a magazine picture of the Eiffel Tower on her desk. She looked at the Eiffel Tower. She looked at Lacey. When Simpson told her to send us in, she nodded at the door and a nerve jumped in her jaw.

Simpson sat in his fat like something cooked.

"My dear Lacey, some brandy, perhaps a sweet liqueur. And Francie needs a sarsaparilla."

"Francine needs nothing. Mr. Simpson, I've come about the car."

"Oh yes, I heard about the fire. Such a misfortune. I'm sure I can be of some help."

Simpson twisted his moustache. Topaz and diamonds choked his little finger. Lacey was impassive; she clutched my hand and left a pale bruise on my wrist. Simpson went on in his honeyed voice.

"J.T. and I were very close, you know. Once I looked after his interests very well. I can do so again."

Lacey was silent. Simpson smiled and watched her. His long black lashes brushed his cheeks, slowly. He blinked once, then again. Opened a drawer in his vast mahogany desk and pulled out a roll of bills. He tossed it in the air, caught it in his fist.

"And there's the matter of that shack property down by the river. Surely you have no illusions that J.T. will ever work the mill again. I know you ran his business those last years; you have the know-how, I have the means. Perhaps we may arrive at a workable situation . . ."

Simpson was sweating now, his hair gleamed pomaded and perfect. He held out the money and Lacey didn't move. I stepped forward and took it.

We put the money in the iron box; Lacey gave up the deed to the mill. I remember J.T. staying in his room, and the sound of the rocking chair creaking for hours as he sat, rocking, with his arms crossed, staring at the wall. Jocasta was not singing. Lacey had locked her door and the house was weighted with silence, sinking in the dark. I fell asleep.

I saw my father standing over me in his checkered cap, red silk scarf, old suede driving coat. He had a pistol in his hand.

"Frank," he said. "It's time to go."

He lifted me so softly I thought I dreamed him. He pulled

nightgown down to cover my thighs and we crept quietly
wn two flights of stairs past the sleepers. Everything slept;
es drooped close to the house, no insects sounded. My fa-
er's face above me took on an ivory cast. The moon was gone
d it was nearly dawn.

At the garage he fired two quick shots at the locks. The sharp
port of the gun echoed back and forth. I saw Lacey's light go
but I was in the car and the car was roaring. J.T. eased it
wn the street and gathered speed. He smiled, his hair blew
ck. The old bridge rattled under us and moved its lamps;
eir twelve whirled reflections wobbled in the river. J.T.
xed his beautiful hands and muttered. He touched the
ther dash and the steering wheel laced with calfskin. We
ent faster out the bridge road to the mill.

"Pop?" I said. "Pop, where we going?"

"Straight home, boy. Straight home."

The motor revved. At top speed the car began to shake. We
ere moving up Tucker Mountain and we shuddered at the
est. A sharp quick crack. I didn't feel myself jump but I saw
e wheel spin off, I saw the black Ford fly off the mountain and
y father's red scarf streaming.

I looked down two ledges at the overturned car. The wheels
hined and smoked. I scrambled down but J.T. was nowhere. I
lled for him, choking on the smell of the car, then I saw him
ove me climbing back to the road. He had the steering wheel
one hand. At the top he turned and looked down.

"Frank," he yelled. "Hurry, it's getting late."

The mill was on the other side of Tucker Mountain. We
alked. The light came up. Mist rose off the river and the rows
empty shacks seemed to float.

"There they are," said J.T. "They're always here this time of
y."

"Who, Pop? Who's here?"

"They are, boy. Look at them, they know who you are."

He raised his arm in the direction of the shacks. His h.
hung limp and crooked.

"Where, Pop?"

"The windows, Frank. Look at the windows."

They were slanted in their rotted sills. Broken glass stood
in jagged angles; what was left pearled at odd curves in
light. Something moved, then I knew it was true; I was as cr
as him. The faces shimmered like they were coming up out
water. They rose up from some place existing alongside
suddenly visible. Their blurry features held the same exp
sion, they moved in and out of each other. Wind rushed, wl
pering sounds I couldn't make out; more and more whisperi
louder and louder . . . then they made one sound. "Francin
they said, "Francine."

"Francine. Francine, come here. Over here."

I saw my mother at the edge of the woods. She had J.T.'s
deer rifle and she had it pointed at him. Beyond her Jocasta
in the delivery cart and didn't look at us. Lacey called me ag
and I tried to move. She fired the gun in the air; while
sharp boom moved around in the trees I ran to her. I knew
faces watched me. J.T. still looked at them, smiling. My motl
held me away from him, tightly, until the faces faded. I m
have talked, I must have said I saw them. Her eyes were h
with light. The butt of the gun pressed into her stomach. S
put J.T. in the cart and tied him in with a thick rope.
smoothed his torn clothes while she walked me through
shacks. Empty, every one of them. Rats thumped across
porches.

After that we had to have him put away. The morning th
came and got him, he turned at the door.

"Lacey," he said calmly, "Aren't you coming with me?"

Solo
Dance

he hadn't been home in a long time. Her father had a cancer
operation; she went home. She went to the hospital every other
day, sitting for hours beside his bed. She could see him flicker-
ing. He was very thin and the skin on his legs was soft and pure
like fine paper. She remembered him saying 'I give up' when
he was angry or exasperated. Sometimes he said it as a joke,
'Jesus Christ, I give up.' She kept hearing his voice in the words
now even though he wasn't saying them. She read his get-well
cards aloud to him. One was from her mother's relatives. Well,
he said, I don't think they had anything to do with it. He was
speaking of his divorce two years before.

She put lather in a hospital cup and he got up to shave in the
mirror. He had to lean on the sink. She combed the back of his

head with water and her fingers. His hair was long after six weeks in the hospital, a gray-silver full of shadow and smudge. She helped him get slowly into bed and he lay against the pillows breathing heavily. She sat down again. I can't wait till I get some weight on me, he said, So I can knock down that son of-a-bitch lawyer right in front of the courthouse.

She sat watching her father. His robe was patterned with tiny horses, sorrels in arabesques. When she was very young, she had started ballet lessons. At the first class her teacher raised her leg until her foot was flat against the wall beside her head. He held it there and looked at her. She looked back at him, thinking to herself it didn't hurt and willing her eyes dry.

Her father was twisting his hands. How's your mother? She must be half crazy by now. She wanted to be by herself and brother that's what she got.

The
Heavenly
Animal

Jancy's father always wanted to fix her car. Every time she came home for a visit, he called her at her mother's house and asked about the car with a second sentence.

Well, he'd say, How are you?

Fine, I'm fine.

And how's the car? Have any trouble?

He became incensed if Jancy's mother answered. He slammed the receiver down and broke the connection. They always knew who it was by the stutter of silence, then the violent click. He lived alone in a house ten blocks away.

Often, he would drive by and see Jancy's car before she'd even taken her coat off. He stopped his aging black Ford on the sloping street and honked two tentative blasts. He hadn't come inside her mother's house since the divorce five years ago. He wouldn't even step on the grass of the block-shaped lawn. This time Jancy saw his car from the bathroom window. She cursed and pulled her pants up. She walked outside and the heavy car door swung open. Her father wore a wool hat with a turned-up brim and small gray feather. Jancy loved the feather.

Hi, she said.

Well, hi there. When did you get in?

About five minutes ago.

Have any trouble?

She got into the car. The black interior was very clean and the empty litter bag hung from the radio knob. Jancy thought she could smell its new plastic mingling with the odor of his cigar. She leaned over and kissed him.

Thank god, she thought, he looks better.

He pointed to her car. What the hell did you do to the chrome along the side there? he said.

Trying to park, Jancy said. Got in a tight spot.

Her father shook his head and grimaced. He held the butt of the cigar with his thumb and forefinger. Jancy saw the flat chewed softness of the butt where he held it in his mouth, and the stain on his lips where it touched.

Jesus, Honey, he said.

Can't win them all.

But you got to win some of them, he said. That car's got to last you a long time.

It will, Jancy said. It's a good car. Like a tank. I could drive that car through the fiery pits of hell and come out smelling like a rose.

Well. Everything you do to it takes money to fix. And I just don't have it.

Don't want it fixed, Jancy said. Works fine without the chrome.

He never asked her at first how long she was going to stay.
For the past few years she'd come home between school terms.
Or from far-flung towns up East, out West. Sometimes during
her visits she left to see friends. He would rant close to her
face, breathing hard.

Why in God's name would you go to Washington, D.C.?
Nothing there but niggers. And what the hell do you want in
New York? You're going to wear out your car. You've driven
that car thirty thousand miles in one year—Why? What the hell
for?

The people I care about are far apart. I don't get many
chances to see them.

Jesus Christ, you come home and off you go.

I'll be back in four days.

That's not the goddamn point. You'll get yourself crippled up
in a car wreck running around like this. Then where will you
be?

Jancy would sigh and feel herself harden.

I won't stay in one place all my life out of fear I'll get crippled
if I move, she'd say.

Well I understand that, but *Jesus*.

His breathing would grow quiet. He rubbed his fingers and
twisted the gold Masonic ring he wore in place of a wedding
band.

Honey, he'd say. You got to *think* of these things.

And they would both sit staring.

Down the street Jancy saw red stop signs and the lawns of
churches. Today he was in a good mood. Today he was just glad
to see her. And he didn't know she was going to see Michael.
Or was she?

What do you think? he said. Do you want to go out for lunch
tomorrow? I go down to the Catholic church there, they have a
senior citizen's meal. Pretty good food.

Jancy smiled. Do you remember when you stopped buying Listerine, she asked, because you found out a Catholic owned the company?

She could tell he didn't remember, but he grinned.

Hell, he said. Damn Catholics own everything.

He was sixty-seven. Tiny blood vessels in his cheeks had burst. There was that redness in his skin, and the blue of shadows, gauntness of the weight loss a year ago. His skin got softer, his eyelids translucent as crepe. His eyelashes were very short and reddish. The flesh drooped under his heavy brows. As a young man, he'd been almost sloe-eyed. Bedroom eyes, her mother called them. Now his eyes receded in the mysterious colors of his face.

OK, Jancy said. Lunch.

She got out of the car and bent to look in at him through the open window.

Hey, she said. You look pretty snappy in that hat.

Tonight her mother would leave after supper for Ohio. Jancy would be alone in the house and she would stare at the telephone. She tore lettuce while her mother broiled the steaks.

I don't know why you want to drive all the way up there at night, Jancy said. Why don't you leave in the morning?

I can make better time at night, her mother said. And besides, the wedding is in two days. Your aunt wanted me to come last week. It's not every day her only daughter gets married, and since you refuse to go to weddings . . .

She paused. They heard the meat crackle in the oven.

I'm sorry to leave when you've just gotten here. I thought you'd be here two weeks ago, and we'd have some time before I left. But you'll be here when I get back.

Jancy looked intently into the salad bowl.

Jancy? asked her mother. Why are you so late getting here? Why didn't you write?

I was just busy . . . finishing the term, packing, subletting the apartment—

You could have phoned.

I didn't want to. I hate calling long-distance. It makes me feel lost, listening to all that static.

That's ridiculous, her mother said. Let's get this table cleared off. I don't know why you always come in and dump everything on the first available spot.

Because I believe in instant relief, Jancy said.

—books, backpack, maps, your purse—

She reached for the books and Jancy's leather purse fell to the floor. Its contents spilled and rolled. She bent to retrieve the mess before Jancy could stop her, picking up small plastic bottles of pills.

What are these? she said. What are you doing with all these pills?

I cleaned out my medicine cabinet and threw all the bottles in my purse. They're pills I've had for years—

Don't you think you better throw them away? You might forget what you're taking.

They're all labeled, Jancy said.

Her mother glanced down.

Dalmane, she said. What's Dalmane?

A sleeping pill.

Why would you need sleeping pills?

Because I have trouble sleeping. Why do you think?

Since when?

I don't know. A long time. Off and on. Will you cut it out with the third degree?

Why can't you sleep?

Because I dream my mother is relentlessly asking me questions.

It's Michael. Michael's thrown you for a loop.

Jancy threw the bottles in her purse and stood up quickly. No, she said, Or yes. We're both upset right now.

He certainly is. You're lucky to be rid of him.

I don't want to be rid of him.

He'll drive you crazy if you're not careful. He's got a screw loose and you know it.

You liked him, Jancy said. You liked him so much it made me angry.

Yes, I liked him. But not after this whole mess started. Calling you cruel because he couldn't have things his way. If he was so in love it would have lasted. Cruel. There's not a cruel bone in your body.

I should never have told you he said those things.

They were silent. Jancy smelled the meat cooking.

Why shouldn't you tell me? her mother asked quietly. If you can't talk to your mother, who can you talk to?

Oh Christ, Jancy said. Nobody. I'm hungry. Let's eat and change the subject.

They sat down over full plates. There was steak when Jancy or her brothers came home. Their mother saved it for weeks, months, in the freezer. The meat sizzled on Jancy's plate and she tried to eat. She looked up. The lines in her mother's face seemed deeper than before, grown in. And she was so thin, so perfectly groomed. Earrings. Creased pants. Silk scarves. A bath at the same time every morning while the *Today* show played the news. At night she rubbed the calluses off her heels carefully with a pumice stone.

She looked at Jancy. What are you doing tomorrow? she asked.

Having lunch at the Catholic church, Jancy said.

That ought to be good. Canned peaches and weepy mashed potatoes. Your father is something. Of course he doesn't speak to me on the street, but I see him drive by here in that black car. Every day. Watching for one of you to come home.

Jancy said nothing.

He looks terrible, her mother said.

He looks better than he did, said Jancy.

That's not saying much. He looked horrible for months. Thinner and thinner, like a walking death. I'd see him downtown. He went to the pool hall every day, always by himself. He never did have any friends.

He did, Jancy said. He told me. In the war.

I don't know. I didn't meet him till after that, when he was nearly forty. By then he never seemed to belong—

I remember that weekend you went away and he moved out, Jancy said. He never belonged in this house. The house he built had such big rooms.

Did you know that house is for sale again? her mother asked. It's changed hands several times.

I didn't know, Jancy said. Let's not talk about it.

Her mother sighed. All right, she said. Let's talk about washing these dishes. I really have to get started.

Mom, Jancy said, I might call Michael.

What for? He's five states away and that's where he ought to be.

I may go up there.

Oh, Jancy.

I have to. I can't just let it end here.

Her mother was silent. They heard a gentle thunder.

Clouding up, Jancy said. You may have rain. Need help with your bags?

The car's already packed.

Well, Jancy said.

Her mother collected maps, parcels, a large white-ribboned present. Jancy heard her moving around and thought of waking at night in the house her father had built, the house in the country. There would be the cornered light from the bathroom in the hall. Her father would walk slowly past in slippers and robe to adjust the furnace. The motor would kick in and grunt its soft hum several times a night. Half asleep, Jancy knew her father was awake. The furnace. They must have been winter nights.

Can you grab this? her mother asked.

Jancy took the present. I'll walk you out, she said.

No, just give it to me. There, I've got it.

Jancy smiled. Her mother took her hand.

You're gutsy, she said. You'll be OK.

Good, said Jancy. It's always great to be OK.

Give me a hug.

Jancy embraced her. How often did someone hold her? Her hair smelled fragrant and dark.

Jancy left the lights off. She took a sleeping pill and lay down on the living room couch. Rain splattered the windows. She imagined her father standing by the dining room table. When he moved out he had talked to her brothers about guns.

One rifle goes, he'd said. One stays. Which do you want?

Jancy remembered cigarette smoke in the room, how it curled between their faces.

It don't make any difference to me, he said. But this one's the best for rabbit.

He fingered change far down in his trouser pockets. One brother asked the other which he wanted. The other said it didn't matter, didn't matter. Finally the youngest took the gun and climbed the steps to his room. Their father walked into the kitchen, murmuring, It'll kill rabbits and birds. And if you go after deer, just use slugs.

Jancy heard water dripping. How long had it gone on? Rain was coming down the chimney. She got up and closed the flue, mopped up the rain with a towel. The pills didn't work anymore. What would she do all night? She was afraid of this house, afraid of all the houses in this town. After midnight they were silent and blank. They seemed abandoned.

She looked at the telephone. She picked up the receiver.

Michael? she said.

She dialed his number. The receiver clicked and snapped.

What number are you calling please?

He's gone, thought Jancy.

Hello? What number—

Jancy repeated the numerals.

That number has been disconnected. There's a new number. Shall I ring it for you?

The plastic dial of the princess phone was transparent and yellowed with light.

Ma'am? Shall I ring it?

Yes, Jancy said.

No one home.

Jancy took a bottle of whiskey off the shelf. She would drink enough to make her sleep. The rain had stopped and the house was still. Light from streetlamps fell through the windows. Jancy watched the deserted town. Heavy elms loomed over the sidewalks. Limbs of trees rose and fell on a night breeze. Their shadows moved on the lit-up surface of the street.

A black car glided by.

Jancy stepped back from the window. Taillights blinked re
as the car turned corners and passed away soundlessly.

She picked up the phone and dialed. She lay in the crampe
hallway while the purr of a connection stopped and started
How did it sound there, ringing in the dark? Loud and empty

Hello?

His voice, soft. When they lived together, he used to stan
looking out the window at the alley late at night. He was nake
and perfect. He watched the Midwestern alleys roll across eigl
city blocks paved in old brick. Telephone poles stood weathere
and alone. Their drooping wires glistened, humming one note
He gripped the wooden frame of the window and stood lookin
centaur, quiet, his flanks whitened in moonlight.

Jancy, he said now. It's you, isn't it.

Jancy wore a skirt and sat in the living room. Her fathe
would pull up outside. She would see him lean to watch th
door of the house, his head inclined toward her. His car shinin
and just washed. His hat. His cigar. His baggy pants bought
the same store downtown for thirty years.

Jancy walked outside to watch for him. She didn't want
jump when the horn sounded. And it suddenly hurt her tha
her father was always waiting.

Did he know their old house was being sold again? He ha
contracted the labor and built it himself. He had designed th
heating system, radiant heat piped under the floors so th
wooden parquet was always warm. He had raised the ceiling
the living room fifteen inches so that the crown of her mother
inherited antique bookcase would fit into it. He was a roa
builder, but those last few years, when Jancy was a teen-age
he'd had a series of bad jobs—selling bulldozers, cars, i

urance—After they'd moved he stopped working al-
ogether . . .

The horn sounded suddenly close and shocked her.

Jancy?

Now why did you do that? I'm standing right here, aren't I?
Are you asleep?

No, I just didn't hear you pull up. But you didn't have to
blare that horn at me. It's loud enough to wake the dead.

Well, he said, I thought you needed waking, standing there
staring into space like a knothead.

Right, said Jancy. She got into the car and he was still smiling. She laughed in spite of herself.

I'm a little early, he said. They don't open at the church till
noon. Do you want to go for a drive?

Where to?

We could drive out the falls road, he said.

That would take them past the old house. The hedges and
trees would be larger than Jancy could believe, lush with new
leaves, and rippling. Her father had planted them all.

I don't think so, said Jancy.

The house is for sale.

I know.

Dumbest thing I ever did was to let your mother talk me into
selling that house.

I don't want to hear about my mother.

I'll hate her for the rest of my life for breaking up our family,
he said, his breathing grown heavy. He scowled and touched
the ridges in the steering wheel.

Jancy leaned back in the seat and watched clouds through the
tinted windshield. Remember when you built roads? she asked.

He waited a moment, then looked over at her and pushed his
hat back. I built a lot of them around here, he said, but the

state don't keep them up anymore. They closed the graveyard
road.

He'd taught her how to drive on that road, a narrow un
painted blacktop that wound under train trestles and throug
the cemetery. He said if she could drive on that road she coul
drive anywhere. He made her go that way, cutting across
blind curve up the sudden hill of the entrance, past the carve
pillars with their lopsided lamps. This way, he'd said, and she'
pulled off onto a gravel path that turned sharply along the cre
of a hill. Tombstones were scattered in the lumpy grass. Fa
below Jancy saw the graveyard road looping west by the river
on through woods to the country towns of Volga and Coalto
and Mud Lick.

Stop here, her father directed. He nodded at a patch
ground. There we are, he said, this is where we'll be.

Jancy was sixteen; she'd stared at him and gripped the steerin
wheel.

All right, he'd said. Back up. Let's see how you do goin
backward.

Now her father started his black Ford and they passed th
clipped lawns of houses. He drove slowly, his cigar in hi
mouth.

What will they have to eat at the church? Jancy asked.

Oh, he said. They publish a menu in the paper. Meat loa
today. Fifty cents a person over sixty. Not bad food. Cooks use
to work up at the junior high. But we don't have to go there
We can go to a restaurant if you want.

No, I'd rather go where you usually go. But are you sure I'
allowed?

Certainly. You're my guest. A dollar for guests.

They pulled into the church parking lot. The doors of the re
center were closed. They sat in the car and waited. Jancy re
membered dances held in this building, how she was thirteen

nd came here to dance with the high school boys. They had
anced until they were wet with sweat, then stepped outside into
he winter air. Girls stood by the lighted door and shivered while
he boys smoked cigarettes, squinting into vaporous trails of
moke rings.

What about your car? asked her father.

What about it?

I'm going to take it up to Smitty's and have him go over it.

No. Doesn't need it. The car is fine. I had it checked—

I've made arrangements with Smitty for today. He's got room
nd we better—

But the last time he fixed it, one of the sparkplugs flew out
hile I was driving on the interstate—

Don't you be taking off on Smitty, her father said. He's done
s a lot of good work on that car. I'm trying to help you. You
on't want my help, why just let me know and I'll bow out any-
me.

Jancy sighed. Her father held his hat in his lap and traced the
int lines of the wool plaid with his fingers.

I appreciate your help, she said. But I don't know if Smitty—

He might have made a mistake that one time, her father said.
ut he usually does real good by us.

Volkswagen buses of old people began to pull up. Drivers
pened the double doors of the vans and rolled up a set of
obile steps. Old ladies appeared with their blond canes and
lack-netted pillbox hats. They stepped out one after another,
miling and peeking about.

Where are the old men? Jancy asked.

I think they die off quicker, her father said. These same old
ames have been coming here ever since I have. They just keep
oving.

* * *

Inside were long rows of Formica tables. Eight or nine elder
people sat at each. There were rows of empty chairs. Wom«
with a cashbox between them sat beside the door. Jancy's fath
put his arm around Jancy's waist and patted her.

This is my daughter, he said.

Well, isn't she pretty? said one of the cashiers. The othe
women nodded and smiled.

Jancy signed the guest book. Under 'address' she wrote '
large.' Her father was waiting at one of the tables. He ha
pulled a chair out for her and was standing behind it, waiting
seat her. The women were watching them, like the circli»
nurses that day at the hospital. Her father lay in bed, his arm
so thin that his elbows seemed too large.

This is my daughter, he'd said to the nurses. She came all th
way from California to see me.

Isn't that nice, they'd said. Is she married?

Hell no, her father had laughed. She's married to me.

Now Jancy felt the chair press up behind her legs and she s«
down. Her father took his hat off and nodded at people acro
the table. She saw that his eyes were alight.

Aren't you going to have to get yourself a summer hat? sh
asked.

I reckon so, he said. I just can't find one I like.

Behind the waist-high counter, Jancy saw the fat cooks spoor
ing peaches onto plates from metal cans. They were big womer
their hair netted in silver nets, faces round and flushed from th
ovens. They passed out cafeteria trays premolded for portions.

I used to eat out of those trays in grade school, Jancy said
Are they going to make us sing 'God Is Great?'

No, her father said. But go ahead if it makes you feel better

He chuckled. The last time they'd eaten together was las
December. Michael had come home with Jancy and they'd gon

t to lunch with her father at the Elks Club. Afterward he had
eld Michael's coat for him and eased it onto his shoulders.
e'd never done that for anyone but his sons. Later he'd asked
er, Are you going to marry this man?

Jancy? Aren't you going to eat? Her father was leaning close
to her, pointing at her plate.

What? Oh. I ate a big breakfast. Here, you eat the rest of
mine.

You should eat, said her father. Your face looks thin. Have
you lost weight?

Maybe a little.

You run around too much. If you'd stay in one place for a
while you'd gain a little weight and look better.

Jancy picked up her fork and put it down. Her father had
always made her uneasy. He went into rages, especially in the
car. If he couldn't pass or the car in front slowed suddenly for a
turn, he'd turn red and curse—Goddammit, you son of a bitch,
he'd say. That's right, you chucklehead—That word 'chucklehead' was his utmost brand of contempt. He said it stressing the
first syllable, fuming like a mad bull.

Jancy? You finished? Ready to go?

Her father pushed his plate away and sat watching her,
touching the rim of his empty glass with a finger. She couldn't
answer him. She knew that she would leave to see Michael.
When she told her father, he would shake his head and stam-
mer as he tried to talk. She got up and started for the door.

Jancy's father burned a coal fire past mid-May. He picked up
a poker and stabbed at white embers clinging to the grate.
Flakes of ash drifted into the room.

How long will you be up there? he asked.

I don't know, she said.

Christ Almighty. What are you doing? If this thing betwee
you and him is over, just forget it. Why go chasing up ther
after him? Let him come here, he knows where you are.

I don't have a place for him to stay.

Why couldn't he stay up at the house with you and you
mother?

Because we don't want to stay with my mother.

He clenched his fists and glowered into the fire. He shook hi
head.

I know you're an adult, he said. But goddammit, Jancy, it'
not right. I don't care what you say. It's not right and it won'
come to no good.

It already *has* come to good, Jancy said. She looked at hir
until he broke their gaze.

Why don't you give it up? he said. Give it up and marry him.

Give what up?

All this running around you're doing. Jesus, Honey, you can'
do this all your life. Aren't you twenty-five this summer? I won'
be here forever. What's going to happen to you?

I don't know, Jancy said. How can I know?

He leaned forward, elbows on knees, and clasped his hands
You need a family, he said. No one will ever help you but you
family.

Maybe not, said Jancy.

She thought of the drive. Moving up the East Coast to Mi
chael. She would arrive and sit in the car, waiting to stop trembling, waiting for twelve hours of hot road and radio talk to g
away. She would want Michael so much and she would be afraic
to go into the house.

She looked up at her father.

I have to do this, she said.

What time are you leaving?

Five A.M.

Does your mother know you're going?

I told her I might.

Well. Come down by and we'll hose off the car.

No, you don't need to get up that early.

I'm always awake by then, he said.

Her father was sitting outside on the porch swing as she drove up. He motioned her to pull into the yard under the buckeye tree. The sky had begun to lighten. The stars were gone. The air was chill, misted. He wore a woolen shirt and the hat with the feather nearly hidden in the brim. Before Jancy could get out of the car he picked up the garden hose and twisted the brass nozzle. Water streamed over the windshield. Jancy watched his wavering form as the water broke and runneled. He held the cigar between his teeth and sprayed the bumpers, the headlights, the long sides of the car. He sprayed each tire, walking, revolving, his hand on his hip, the hat pulled low. His face was gentle and gaunt. He would get sicker. Jancy touched her eyes, her mouth. A resignation welled up like tears. He was there and then he was made of moving lines as water flew into the glass. The water stopped slowly.

Jancy got out of the car and they stood looking up at a sky toned the coral of flesh.

It's a long way, he said. You'll get there while it's light?

Yes, Jancy said. Don't worry.

The car sat dripping and poised.

It looks good, Jancy said. I'm taking off in style.

She got in and rolled the window down. Her father came close.

Turn the motor on, he said, then nodded, satisfied at the

growl of the engine. Above them the buckeye spread out gree
and heavy.

When are the buckeyes ripe? Jancy asked.

Not till August.

Can you eat them?

Nope, her father laughed. Buckeyes don't do a thing, don
have a use in the world.

He bent down and kissed her.

Take your time, he said. Go easy.

She drove fast the first few hours. The sun looked like th
moon, dim, layered over. Morning fog burned off slowly. Mar
land mountains were thick and dipped in pockets of fog. Woo
stretched on both sides of the road. Sometimes from a
overpass Jancy saw straggled neon lights still burning in a sm
town. No cars on the highway; she was alone, she ate up th
empty ribbon of the road.

She drove up over a rise and suddenly, looming out of th
mist, the deer was there. She saw the sexual lines of its hea
and long neck. It moved into her, lifted like a flying horse. Sh
swerved. The arching body hit the fender with a final thud an
bounced again, hard, into the side of the car. Jancy looke
through the rearview mirror and saw the splayed form skiddin
back along the berm of the road, bouncing twice in slow mo
tion, twirling and stopping.

The road seemed to close like a tunnel. The look of the deer
head, the beginning arch of the body, was all around Jancy. Sh
seemed to see through the image into the tunneling road. Sh
heard, close to her ear, the soft whuff of the large head ben
over grass, tearing the long grass with its teeth.

She pulled off the road. I should go back and see what I'v

ne, she thought. She turned the motor off. She felt she was
ll moving, and the road shifted into three levels. Wet grass of
e road banks was lush. The road shimmered; one plane of it
ted and moved sideways into the other. Jancy gripped the
nyl seat of the car. She was sinking. The door wouldn't open
d she slid across to get out the other side. She stood up in the
ol air and there was total silence. Jancy tried to walk. The
rth and the asphalt were spongy. She moved around the car
d saw first the moonish curve of the dented fender. The door
as crumpled where the deer had bounced back and slammed
to her. Jancy imagined its flanks, the hard mounds of its
mp. The sheen of it. She staggered and stepped back. The
dden cushion of the grass surprised her and she fell. She saw
en the sweep of short hairs glistening along the length of the
r. The door handle was packed and smeared with golden
es.

There was really nowhere to go.

Once it was Christmas Day. They were driving from home,
om the house her father had built in the country. A deer
mped the road in front of them, clearing the snow, the pave-
ent, the fences of the fields, in two bounds. Beyond its arc the
lls rumpled in snow. The narrow road wound through white
eadows, across the creek, and on. Her father was driving. Her
others had shining play pistols with leather holsters. Her
other wore clip-on earrings of tiny wreaths. They were all
essed in new clothes, and they moved down the road through
e trees.

Happy

She knew if she loved him she could make him happy, but she didn't. Or she did, but it sank into itself like a hole and curled up content. Surrounded by the blur of her own movements, the thought of making him happy was very dear to her. She moved it from place to place, a surprise she never opened. She slept alone at night, soul of a naked priest in her sweet body. Small soft hands, a bread of desire rising in her stomach. When she lay down with the man she loved and didn't, the man opened and opened. Inside him an acrobat tumbled over death. And walked thin wires with nothing above or below. She cried, he was so beautiful in his scarlet tights and white face the size of a dime.

Stars

All winter in Florida he poked his cane at calcified dog turds and swore. In summers he sat on the porch in West Virginia, yelling for the fly swatter and shooting at groundhogs in his fields across the road; so proud of the girl he fathered at sixty. Jit! he yelled, Jitterbugger! Bring the swatter out here!

That summer she was nine. We read *Star Parade* in a tiny back bedroom strung with ribbons from horse shows in the forties. I was a little older but she was taller, her eyes were cerulean and her legs were freckled. When he dies we won't come back here anymore, she said, and her mother, a heavy woman in her fifties with shoulder-length white hair and those same pure eyes, spent afternoons in town. Jit had to sweep the linoleum floors with a broom. He spat in a bucket and she emptied it. We went behind the house to pick mint for his pitchers of ice water; she cracked the ice trays in the sink and cursed him in even tones. He was deaf and couldn't hear unless she yelled. Lazy Jitterbug? he shouted. Where's my water? The sparse white hairs on his concave chest were damp and he wiped his armpits with a towel. Here, you old buzzard, she said. What's that? he asked, and watched her lips. Sir, she said. Yes sir.

Finally he went to sleep in the room with the double bed. We walked up to the snake pit on the winding cow paths and threw pebbles at copperheads coiled on the rocks. Cows gathered farther down at the trough, licking the salt block to a bulging oval. Sometimes she walked, slow motion, into their midst, then turned up her head and screamed. They jerked, stumbling away, and rolled their broad eyes like palsied girls.

When the heat was worst we slipped through the double doors of the old garage. The mossy walls were covered with license plates of dead Mercurys and photos of their ghostly two-tone fins. Burlap bags of feed, torn lawn furniture, hoses and pieces of cars; a radio that played Top Ten at three in the afternoon. We lay on a cot pretending we were Troy Donahue and Sandra Dee, touching each other's stomachs and never pulling our pants down. The Lettermen did billowing movie themes. There's a summer place, they sang. Where our hearts. Will know. All our hopes. She put her face on my chest. You be the boy now, she whispered. Insects got caught in the warm putty of the windows and horseflies drifted up and down the panes. They were furry and weighted, blunt, and their heads were blue.

In winter she sent me her picture and wrote letters. Just because you're a year older than me, her last one said, is no reason not to answer.

The
Patron

I'm fine until he coughs. Then I head for the bathroom. I might grab the chamber pot under his chair and carry its sloshing contents in my flight. I might sprout wings, nearly run up the dark hall holding a squat chalice engraved with angels. His tiled bathroom smells of churches. Incense he asks me to buy and burn there in pewter trays. He doesn't know I get it cheap from the Krishna nuts on a corner just outside his Second Avenue mausoleum—spend the rest at Harry's Peek-A-Boo when my shift is done. And think all day about my favorite films as he pukes and scratches and changes soap operas with a button.

It's the coughing I can't stand. I run and leave him fumbling for Kleenexes, endless powder-blue sheets, gagging finally in a crescendo that leaves him exhausted. Wobbling his little blue head from heaped white cashmere in winter, pastel silks in summer. Wobbling, his eyes unfocused, lighting yet another Silva-Thin. He doesn't mind that I run, terrified, from his hacking fits. He only wishes I'd come back in time to light his thin cigarettes, all four packs a day of them. Bend over him with the sterling silver table lighter, cocked just so in my palm. Croon there we go, there now, as his dappled bald head moves up and down. Sucking, snorting, sniffing. As though he suffocates through slender tubes, filters the color of palominos. Sputtering. There now.

Maybe I'm his goddamn son. He cops an incestuous thrill as I gather his bones together, wrap him up, deposit him in his blue suede chair. You think I'm kidding. No, it's a blue suede chair, sky blue. He sits there on the verge of speech as I strip his bed, peeling fragrant wet sheets from the plastic guard underneath. His piss is not piss, he drinks only mineral water and produces a cloudy chartreuse flow that smells of summer grass.

His night nurse has raised the shades halfway, so the 8 A.M. sun cascades through leaded glass. Casting knots of light on my hair, my chest. I snap the dry white sheets; they billow out over red tulips pulsing in mahogany casements of his windows. Ah James, he whispers. How are you James?

I tell myself I have it easy. He'll die and leave me something, anything. The truth is he'll outlast me by five years, like he outlasts all the rest. In two years I've seen four crowds of them come and go. His boys. His muscular neurotic boys in Danskins and determined eyes. Waiting in the foyer with the marble lions while I oil his drying skin, button him into linen shirts, silk scarves and diamond stickpin the likeness of a locust. Plant him banked in tulips, snapdragons, dark wood and Turkish rugs where he receives them. The French one kissed his wrist on its bald blue vein. The Orientals bowed. The black ones have a sheen like ebony, their biceps ripple. Long muscles in their legs turn and flex in white trousers, gathered at the waist to blouse on molded hips. They smell of herbs. Walk poised on balls of their feet like leopards, big loose cats. They come and go, commit suicide, move to Paris, leave New York for a San Fran mime troupe. Or they overdo it with the big H, shooting up in the ass to preserve their trackless arms.

It's no secret he thinks I'm one of them. He buys my clothes in the same places, wants me to take lessons with their teachers. The Dance, he says. Dancers appear once a week, singly. One of them carries a bamboo cane with a brass mosquito inlaid in its ivory tip. He wants what he sees but he is calm, he is nearly disguised. He tells me no, the old man was never a dancer. Some lover he followed around, who knows. There are stories. He taps the blond cane once, he smiles at me. He asks me where I study. I study at Harry's Peek-A-Boo. He nods, leans back against the velvet wallpaper. How is old Harry? In leaner days they starred, all of them, in some of Harry's films; Harry fancies himself the porno avant-garde. But I never watch those films.

I watch the old ones. The ones in machines for a quarter. Put your face to the lens, a binocular of secrets. 1940s and '50s. Kinks were subtle and women were always alone; climbing ladders and bending over long finned cars. How beautiful they were, breasts the size of oranges, powdered brows. Glistening lips so dark they look black in black and white, shining like rain on night streets. And they were so modestly teasing, smiling their serious smiles. So innocent you can't think of them that way.

There's the blond whose cheeks look bruised with rouge, kneeling beside a bathtub and scrubbing it out with a long brush. She's wrapped in a towel, her permed hair falling in her eyes as she stretches to swipe the drain, makes a circle with her mouth. She turns on the water and gets up awkwardly, slipping the cloth below her breasts. Says Oh as they emerge, catches the towel in the vee of her crotch. Turns as the camera pulls back to get what you must call her derriere. Her long white thighs, her shaven calves, her ankles, her ever-present black spike heels. It ends, like all of them, before it is over. She moving as though to step in . . . You can't believe she's being paid.

In her shoes, I tell Harry. They never take off their shoes.

Kid, yr a case, says Harry. You really got a case.

He is sorting his sodomy postcards, animals mostly, and eat-- ing a tuna-on-rye. He's been here fifteen years, keeps free cof- fee in the back and reuses the plastic cups. The film stalls smell of his cigars. His plastic-covered magazines are layered over with dust and fine plaster. Harry says he'll die in his chair, a high stool with a back and doughnut cushion. Harry has a bad prostate. He'll end up dribbling too, but he doesn't think about it.

See ya kid, says Harry. He's talking to himself before I'm out the door. What a case, he says to the empty store.

I watch the old man's fingers. They are the size and color of varnished chopsticks. They flutter imperceptibly, like antennae. Then he begins to cough.

Once a month his boys perform. I wheel him to the drawing

oom. Lilies and jade trees. Polished floor. He sits in a rapture
diapers and clamp, wrapped in Colombian blankets, as his
ancers leap on supple legs. Swirling, arching arms, straight
es touching floor in quick half-snaps. They move one by one
cross his range of vision; pliés, grands jetés. Their eyes fix on
e unseen; they dive and come back to it, magnetized. They
ome back to it, even music can't conceal that they are slaves.
mooth and perfect but shaking, muscles a hidden vibrato. And
vhen they finish they are drenched. Eyes still focused, point of
ght in the pupil like they are hurt with something sharp and
naking room. They stand panting, each pectoral a hard and glis-
ening oval under skin. They heave, shining. They drip.

He grips my hand. As I wheel him back to his room I smell
is sweat rise, pure as wet fruit. The dancers stand motionless
ehind us; the long hall is still and rose under its stained-glass
ome. His room is shadowed. I have drawn the tapestried
rapes until one slit of light falls through to waste on the parquet floor. He mumbles words I can't quite hear, a name I
von't recognize. His eyes retain that focus stolen from the
ance, so wide, his amethyst eyes. Iris purely violet in a yellow
queous. He stares, begins the name. I lay him out in the dark-
ned room. Take away his silken clothes, his jewels, his linen
underwear. His diapers, the clamp enclosing his penis; a penis
ale, very soft, uncut in its fragile hood. I sponge him with
lcohol and scented water. Stroke his small body as it cools, the
ones thinly covered in a flesh almost transparent. I see their
hadows holding still beneath his skin like something under-
vater.

Every morning. He is there, the wide bed stretching around
im like a room. Bruno, the big night nurse, has fed him his

yogurt and strained pears. A nectar pulverized to mush
Bruno, who cooks and cleans and walks unbending; a tree
legs. Bruno, his globular arms, his Roman nose, his tight ceda
colored curls. He is a brute with a sensual mouth, liftin
weights in his rooms on the third floor. He is never far awa
Disappears for my eight hours and returns, ready with tig
balm in an etched brass box and small rubber balls to exerci
the old man's skeletal hands.

Evenings. Bruno nods once as I pull on my coat, make for th
door. The old man reaches for him but his violet eyes follow n
around the bed, the chair, the massive closet door opening wi
a clean swish. Rustling of hangers sewn in padded silk, padde
blue silk. His violet eyes turning, watching, sucking strange an
tentative at my arms. Then the voice, faintly. James . . . ta
care . . . James, have you plans for the evening . . . I am fl
ing through the hallway, down the banistered stairs past froze
lions, through double doors carved with gods and snakes, an
the static knockers shaped in cold brass crows. Already Bruno
rolling those red balls in the yellow palms, moving the aurea
fingers, the flaxen arms stripped of cover. And I am opening th
orange door to Harry's Peek-A-Boo.

Harry's layered toupee, his beady face, appear between th
shelves. He wobbles toward me, happy, on his sequined pla
form shoes. Hi ya kid. Harry gives me thick black coffee lace
with Jack Daniel's, brewing since noon. He touches my shou
der, says he's got some new films in, those goofy ones I lik
collector's items. Just my style, not a cunt shows in the bunc
Look here kid.

The old film curls apart in his hands, cracked along the edg
where tiny holes of light appear. Shaking a little in his finger

his small thick hands. Hands of a fat child with a tremor. He loads the machine and tosses me a quarter.

Volleyball by the high seawall. San Diego, 1942. She is standing by the net; she is going to play alone. No, she is only walking, her black hair waved and blown to expose her neck. She drops her eyes, painted lashes, looks up as the camera pulls away. She is told to turn, toss the ball into the wavering net. Striped, bouncing off, it rolls into the surf. Stripes seemingly unwinding across the sand. A round pinwheel, and she is slowly after it. Laughing, pulling the loose bow of her bra until it drops. Struggling a little in the waves, the incoming tide. Turning to kick water at the camera, and her foot emerges bare as the shoe flies off. She lunges for it. Pasted wet hair shows her round face rounder, wartime starlet eyes a little slanted. Her expression strives to make them wider, not so black. She is falling into a corner of the frame, and there, where she has entered, the ocean starts to burn. A flat amoeba shape eats up the film.

Sorry kid. Damn films get hot in the machine, too old. Have a sandwich. Harry sits in the front, eating. Rubbing his wrinkled face. His store window sees the whole corner, the cars and changing lights. Krishnas dancing in their orange clothes to catch the rush-hour traffic, and the old man's house rising above its wall. That wrought-iron balcony on the second floor, the sun going down.

At sunset Bruno picks him up, holds him twenty minutes or so by the window. I see them now, outside on the balcony though it is only early spring. Old man just a swaddled bundle, no head, and Bruno a dark shape.

Harry wipes his hands on his pants and winks. Queers, he says, I love em. Perv fairies. Happens all over when the sun goes down.

I think of them. At night. I believe he sits on Bruno's lap, wrapped in those big arms and several blankets. They never

speak. They watch television until the picture fades to one
burning spot the size of an eye.

I hold back just enough. He puts out a hundred a week for
prescriptions, vitamins, imported Korean ginseng, papaya root,
subtle sleeping powders, exotic capsules of pure oxygen. He
writes me a check, I buy them all. Overcharge him just enough
and keep the difference. Make and label some of them myself,
pills of sugar, dried lemon peel, peppermint in a clear digest-
ible shell. Or I dye them bright colors so they range in my
hands like rainbows. Offer them on cut-glass trays, tip the gob-
let to his lips. And he swallows, thirsting for tropics, the juice of
the mango. His vitamins sit waiting in clear cannisters, delicate
in cotton and glass. I switch them, give them to him in strange
bottles, pretend to buy them twice. The violet eyes grow more
luminous, the skull almost visible in the bald head.
I could fence his rings and bracelets at Harry's, there are
boxes he ignores. He is too thin to wear them, he is uncon-
cerned. Emeralds, rubies, opals gleam unseen. Moonstones
glow in the dark. And his bracelets, Indian, Egyptian gold, old
turquoise, tooled Irani silver. All neglected. Even the necklaces. He says he cannot breathe beneath the faintest gold
chains, smallest pearls, jeweled chips tiny as grass seed. They
oppress him.
Only the locust, heavy emblazoned diamond on its stemmed
gold pin. He asks for it repeatedly. I fasten light silk scarves
around his throat, locust burning a fiery head large as the nail of
my smallest finger. Nestling in the cloth. Ruby eyes, the
studded wings, the thin gold legs curled so they disappear.
He believes I admire the locust. As he sleeps, long afternoons, I open the drawer beside his bed to watch it. Jewel in

dark brocade. The gold set is true to the insect, that single particle of ravages and swarms. Winged grasshopper, pestilence. Its head flawless, diamond, the thin gold tongue protruding, and lo··· ·, the segmented legs. I want to take it, hide it in my clot! ¦ not come back. In the drawer the locust glints and almos. ..oves.

I touch it. From the bed a wheezing sigh, an exhalation that catches on itself and chokes. I jerk, my finger barely touching the head of the jewel, the brilliant thorax. The old man rolls, wakened, but I look again and the locust's head is faintly smeared. A prong of the setting is loose and jagged. My finger, the stinging. I suck the blood away and shut the drawer.

In summer the street gets hot. Heat wavers from its surface and the Krishnas dance, jerking thin skirts dark in sweated patches. Jingling ankle bells. Leathery feet, thud, calluses so deep tiny worms lay eggs in their cracks.

But his stone house is cool, the street a muffled hum. Bruno rigs his bed with a clear tent and a metal tube of oxygen. We keep the tent rolled up until he sleeps and then we lower it, Bruno's perfect hands soundless on its plastic walls. Inside the old man sleeps with his eyes open; veiled in a clear dry veil.

At noon I prop him in a chair and wrap him up, feel his heart knocking in his ribs like something trying to hatch. Cover his legs with soft wools, his feet in cowhide slippers, golden, lined in gold. His feet are too long for his bony¯ankles, the peaked shank bones of his legs. His toes seem longer than fingers, their nails thick, manicured, embossed with blue half-moons and a natural sheen. As I fit the slippers his toes rise together, once, poised like the hand of some intelligent damaged creature.

* * *

Hey kid, whaddya know? Harry gets a little fatter every su
mer. Points to his line of quarter machines. Antiques, he sa
Every one of em, found out last week. He crows, says he's
some valuable property here. He grins.

In summer the store is hot, old dirt in the floors smells o
Only his dedicated customers appear. Overhead the old ceil
fans whirr and buzz. Black points in the center, a blur of blad

I don't come every night. Only sometimes. Watch the ho
from Harry's streaked window, watch the corner close do
and turn crazy.

Harry shakes his head at me. Kid, he says. Yr getting skinn
Yr losing weight kid.

The old man is always cool, pale as a root. Once a day there
the walk to the bathroom, clump of the aluminum walker a
slow scud of his feet behind. He can't go the whole distan
this week I carry him from the bathroom door to the toil
Floor an endless series of marble dots.

A dancer's thin support bar runs along the wall. Last year
walked up and down its length grasping the metal, jerking
legs along. Once he fell, broke his ankles. They mended bad
they hobble him, inching, tottering. Like a Chinese girl w
bound feet; a girl of good family whose feet are the feet o
baby.

Bathroom. Wide, marble, windows wavy and leaded. Lig
so dim the crickets sing all day. They hang in tiny cages fr
the ceiling, suspended by strings of prismed beads. There is
skylight, but the ragged palms have grown so tall they diffu
the sun.

I carry him, he begins to shake. A spasm beginning; I want to put him on the toilet and leave, wait in the hall as always until he presses the call bell, chimes his strange high note. The toilet has a padded back and sides, he is strapped in, he won't topple over as the coughing progresses. Waiting, I try not to hear, frightened, clenched—the scraping, the shuddered hacks, the yellowed phlegm he drools. It smells of his disease, deep, damp. Not lilies and silks, mahogany, blond bamboo. It is this smell, putrid, comes out of him. I wait, outside in the long hall.

Today I put him down and draw away. But he has clutched my wrist. Yellow fingers tight, pressing, I shake them, pull, finally try to pry them off. Panic, think . . . this strength, involuntary . . . a stroke? . . . but then I see his face. The eyes recognize. Escaping them I look down, the floor. There is blood, trickles of it from his hand, his drawn white fist. He lets go; his palm opens. Couched in his thin flesh, the locust has eaten a small gash with its jagged gold. It drops to the floor and rolls, glittering. Yours, he says. The spasm builds, he shakes to hold it back. Skin around his eyes so white it seems to glow, and there are tears. Sounds. He releases me.

I step back but he is whispering. I am drawn to him, closer. His violet eyes and the whispers, a name. Closer. He beckons, frail hand turning like a leaf. I bend, his fluttering lips at my ear. He wheezes, breath a rotted weight; yet from his skin there is a light perfume, drying of an ancient herb. He whispers, softer. Love, my love, he whispers. Don't leave me.

Strangers
in the Night

Like everyone else, she thought a lot about eating and sleeping. When she was sleeping she felt like death floating free, a white seed over the water. Eating, she thought about sex and chewed pears as though they were conscious. When she was making love she felt she was dancing in a churning water, floating, but attached to something else. Once she almost died and went so far she saw how free the planet floated, how it is only a shadow, and was frightened back to herself. Later, when she explained this to him, he put his arms around her. She thought she had come home and they were in a shadow, dancing.

Souvenir

Kate always sent her mother a card on Valentine's Day. She timed the mails from wherever she was so that the cards arrived on February 14th. Her parents had celebrated the day in some small fashion, and since her father's death six years before, Kate made a gesture of compensatory remembrance. At first, she made the cards herself: collage and pressed grasses on construction paper sewn in fabric. Now she settled for art reproductions, glossy cards with blank insides. Kate wrote in them with colored inks, "You have always been my Valentine," or simply "Hey, take care of yourself." She might enclose a present as well, something small enough to fit into an envelope; a sachet, a perfumed soap, a funny tintype of a prune-faced man in a bowler hat.

This time, she forgot. Despite the garish displays of paper
cupids and heart-shaped boxes in drugstore windows, she let
the day nearly approach before remembering. It was too late to
send anything in the mail. She called her mother long-distance
at night when the rates were low.

"Mom? How are you?"

"It's you! How are *you*?" Her mother's voice grew suddenly
brighter; Kate recognized a tone reserved for welcome company. Sometimes it took a while to warm up.

"I'm fine," answered Kate. "What have you been doing?"

"Well, actually I was trying to sleep."

"Sleep? You should be out setting the old hometown on fire."

"The old hometown can burn up without me tonight."

"Really? What's going on?"

"I'm running in-service training sessions for the primary
teachers." Kate's mother was a school superintendent. "They're
driving me batty. You'd think their brains were rubber."

"They are," Kate said. "Or you wouldn't have to train them.
Think of them as a salvation, they create a need for your job."

"Some salvation. Besides, your logic is ridiculous. Just because someone needs training doesn't mean they're stupid."

"I'm just kidding. But *I'm* stupid. I forgot to send you a Valentine's card."

"You did? That's bad. I'm trained to receive one. They bring
me luck."

"You're receiving a phone call instead," Kate said. "Won't
that do?"

"Of course," said her mother, "but this is costing you money.
Tell me quick, how are you?"

"Oh, you know. Doctoral pursuits. Doing my student try,
grooving with the professors."

"The professors? You'd better watch yourself."

"It's a joke, Mom, a joke. But what about you? Any men on the horizon?"

"No, not really. A married salesman or two asking me to dinner when they come through the office. Thank heavens I never let those things get started."

"You should do what you want to," Kate said.

"Sure," said her mother. "And where would I be then?"

"I don't know. Maybe Venezuela."

"They don't even have plumbing in Venezuela."

"Yes, but their sunsets are perfect, and the villages are full of dark passionate men in blousy shirts."

"That's your department, not mine."

"Ha," Kate said, "I wish it were my department. Sounds a lot more exciting than teaching undergraduates."

Her mother laughed. "Be careful," she said. "You'll get what you want. End up sweeping a dirt floor with a squawling baby around your neck."

"A dark baby," Kate said, "to stir up the family blood."

"Nothing would surprise me," her mother said as the line went fuzzy. Her voice was submerged in static, then surfaced. "Listen," she was saying. "Write to me. You seem so far away."

They hung up and Kate sat watching the windows of the neighboring house. The curtains were transparent and flowered and none of them matched. Silhouettes of the window frames spread across them like single dark bars. Her mother's curtains were all the same, white cotton hemmed with a ruffle, tiebacks blousing the cloth into identical shapes. From the street it looked as if the house was always in order.

Kate made a cup of strong Chinese tea, turned the lights off, and sat holding the warm cup in the dark. Her mother kept no real tea in the house, just packets of instant diabetic mixture which tasted of chemical sweetener and had a bitter aftertaste.

The packets sat on the shelf next to her mother's miniature scales. The scales were white. Kate saw clearly the face of the metal dial on the front, its markings and trembling needle. Her mother weighed portions of food for meals: frozen broccoli, slices of plastic-wrapped Kraft cheese, careful chunks of roast beef. A dog-eared copy of *The Diabetic Diet* had remained propped against the salt shaker for the last two years.

Kate rubbed her forehead. Often at night she had headaches. Sometimes she wondered if there were an agent in her body, a secret in her blood making ready to work against her.

The phone blared repeatedly, careening into her sleep. Kate scrambled out of bed, naked and cold, stumbling, before she recognized the striped wallpaper of her bedroom and realized the phone was right there on the bedside table, as always. She picked up the receiver.

"Kate?" said her brother's voice. "It's Robert. Mom is in the hospital. They don't know what's wrong but she's in for tests."

"Tests? What's happened? I just talked to her last night."

"I'm not sure. She called the neighbors and they took her to the emergency room around dawn." Robert's voice still had that slight twang Kate knew was disappearing from her own. He would be calling from his insurance office, nine o'clock their time, in his thick glasses and wide, perfectly knotted tie. He was a member of the million-dollar club and his picture, tiny, the size of a postage stamp, appeared in the Mutual of Omaha magazine. His voice seemed small too over the distance. Kate felt heavy and dulled. She would never make much money, and recently she had begun wearing make-up again, waking smeared mascara as she had in high school.

"Is Mom all right?" she managed now. "How serious is it?"

"They're not sure," Robert said. "Her doctor thinks it could have been any of several things, but they're doing X rays."

"Her doctor *thinks?* Doesn't he know? Get her to someone else. There aren't any doctors in that one-horse town."

"I don't know about that," Robert said defensively. "Anyway, I can't force her. You know how she is about money."

"Money? She could have a stroke and drop dead while her doctor wonders what's wrong."

"Doesn't matter. You know you can't tell her what to do."

"Could I call her somehow?"

"No, not yet. And don't get her all worried. She's been scared enough as it is. I'll tell her what you said about getting another opinion, and I'll call you back in a few hours when I have some news. Meanwhile, she's all right, do you hear?"

The line went dead with a click and Kate walked to the bathroom to wash her face. She splashed her eyes and felt guilty about the Valentine's card. Slogans danced in her head like reprimands. *For A Special One. Dearest Mother. My Best Friend.* Despite Robert, after breakfast she would call the hospital.

She sat a long time with her coffee, waiting for minutes to pass, considering how many meals she and her mother ate alone. Similar times of day, hundreds of miles apart. Women by themselves. The last person Kate had eaten breakfast with had been someone she'd met in a bar. He was passing through town. He liked his fried eggs gelatinized in the center, only lightly runny, and Kate had studiously looked away as he ate. The night before he'd looked down from above her as he finished and she still moved under him. "You're still wanting," he'd said. "That's nice." Mornings now, Kate saw her own face in the mirror and was glad she'd forgotten his name. When she looked at her reflection from the side, she saw a faint etching of lines beside her mouth. She hadn't slept with anyone for five weeks, and the skin beneath her eyes had taken on a creamy darkness.

She reached for the phone but drew back. It seemed bad luck to ask for news, to push toward whatever was coming as though she had no respect for it.

Standing in the kitchen last summer, her mother had stirred gravy and argued with her.

"I'm thinking of your own good, not mine," she'd said. "Think of what you put yourself through. And how can you feel right about it? You were born here, I don't care what you say." Her voice broke and she looked, perplexed, at the broth in the pan.

"But, hypothetically," Kate continued, her own voice unaccountably shaking, "if I'm willing to endure whatever I have to, do you have a right to object? You're my mother. You're supposed to defend my choices."

"You'll have enough trouble without choosing more for yourself. Using birth control that'll ruin your insides, moving from one place to another. I can't defend your choices. I can't even defend myself against you." She wiped her eyes on a napkin.

"Why do you have to make me feel so guilty?" Kate said, fighting tears of frustration. "I'm not attacking you."

"You're not? Then who are you talking to?"

"Oh Mom, give me a break."

"I've tried to give you more than that," her mother said. "I know what your choices are saying to me." She set the steaming gravy off the stove. "You may feel very differently later on. It just a shame I won't be around to see it."

"Oh? Where will you be?"

"Floating around on a fleecy cloud."

Kate got up to set the table before she realized her mother had already done it.

The days went by. They'd gone shopping before Kate left. Standing at the cash register in an antique shop on Main Street, they bought each other pewter candle holders. "A souvenir," her mother said. "A reminder to always be nice to yourself. If you live alone you should eat by candlelight."

"Listen," Kate said, "I eat in a heart-shaped tub with bubbles to my chin. I sleep on satin sheets and my mattress has a built-in massage engine. My overnight guests are impressed. You don't have to tell me about the solitary pleasures."

They laughed and touched hands.

"Well," her mother said. "If you like yourself, I must have done something right."

Robert didn't phone until evening. His voice was fatigued and thin. "I've moved her to the university hospital," he said. "They can't deal with it at home."

Kate waited, saying nothing. She concentrated on the toes of her shoes. They needed shining. *You never take care of anything,* her mother would say.

"She has a tumor in her head." He said it firmly, as though Kate might challenge him.

"I'll take a plane tomorrow morning," Kate answered, "I'll be there by noon."

Robert exhaled. "Look," he said, "don't even come back here unless you can keep your mouth shut and do it my way."

"Get to the point."

"The point is they believe she has a malignancy and we're not going to tell her. I almost didn't tell you." His voice faltered. "They're going to operate but if they find what they're expecting, they don't think they can stop it."

For a moment there was no sound except an oceanic vibration of distance on the wire. Even that sound grew still. Robert breathed. Kate could almost see him, in a booth at the hospital, staring straight ahead at the plastic instructions screwed to the narrow rectangular body of the telephone. It seemed to her that she was hurtling toward him.

"I'll do it your way," she said.

The hospital cafeteria was a large room full of orange Formica tables. Its southern wall was glass. Across the highway, Kate saw a small park modestly dotted with amusement rides and bordered by a narrow band of river. How odd, to build a children's park across from a medical center. The sight was pleasant in a cruel way. The rolling lawn of the little park was perfectly, relentlessly green.

Robert sat down. Their mother was to have surgery in two days.

"After it's over," he said, "they're not certain what will happen. The tumor is in a bad place. There may be some paralysis."

"What kind of paralysis?" Kate said. She watched him twist the green-edged coffee cup around and around on its saucer.

"Facial. And maybe worse."

"You've told her this?"

He didn't answer.

"Robert, what is she going to think if she wakes up and—"

He leaned forward, grasping the cup and speaking through clenched teeth. "Don't you think I thought of that?" He gripped the sides of the table and the cup rolled onto the carpeted floor with a dull thud. He seemed ready to throw the table after it, then grabbed Kate's wrists and squeezed them hard.

"You didn't drive her here," he said. "She was so scared she couldn't talk. How much do you want to hand her at once?"

Kate watched the cup sitting solidly on the nubby carpet.

"We've told her it's benign," Robert said, "that the surgery will cause complications, but she can learn back whatever is lost."

Kate looked at him. "Is that true?"

"They hope so."

"We're lying to her, all of us, more and more." Kate pulled her hands away and Robert touched her shoulder.

"What do *you* want to tell her, Kate? 'You're fifty-five and you're done for'?"

She stiffened. "Why put her through the operation at all?"

He sat back and dropped his arms, lowering his head. "Because without it she'd be in bad pain. Soon." They were silent, then he looked up. "And anyway," he said softly, "we don't *know*, do we? She may have a better chance than they think."

Kate put her hands on her face. Behind her closed eyes she saw a succession of blocks tumbling over.

They took the elevator up to the hospital room. They were alone and they stood close together. Above the door red numerals lit up, flashing. Behind the illuminated shapes droned an impersonal hum of machinery.

Then the doors opened with a sucking sound. Three nurses stood waiting with a lunch cart, identical covered trays stacked in tiers. There was a hot bland smell, like warm cardboard. One of the women caught the thick steel door with her arm and smiled. Kate looked quickly at their rubber-soled shoes. White polish, the kind that rubs off. And their legs seemed only white shapes, boneless and two-dimensional, stepping silently into the metal cage.

She looked smaller in the white bed. The chrome side rails were pulled up and she seemed powerless behind them, her dark hair pushed back from her face and her forearms delicate in the baggy hospital gown. Her eyes were different in some nearly imperceptible way; she held them wider, they were shiny with a veiled wetness. For a moment the room seemed empty of all else; there were only her eyes and the dark blossoms of the flowers on the table beside her. Red roses with pine. Everyone had sent the same thing.

Robert walked close to the bed with his hands clasped behind his back, as though afraid to touch. "Where did all the flowers come from?" he asked.

"From school, and the neighbors. And Katie." She smiled.

"FTD," Kate said. "Before I left home. I felt so bad for not being here all along."

"That's silly," said their mother. "You can hardly sit at home and wait for some problem to arise."

"Speaking of problems," Robert said, "the doctor tells me you're not eating. Do I have to urge you a little?" He sat down on the edge of the bed and shook the silverware from its paper sleeve.

Kate touched the plastic tray. "Jell-O and canned cream of chicken soup. Looks great. We should have brought you something."

"They don't *want* us to bring her anything," Robert said. "This is a hospital. And I'm sure your comments make her lunch seem even more appetizing."

"I'll eat it!" said their mother in mock dismay. "Admit they sent you in here to stage a battle until I gave in."

"I'm sorry," Kate said. "He's right."

Robert grinned. "Did you hear that? She says I'm right. I don't believe it." He pushed the tray closer to his mother's chest and made a show of tucking a napkin under her chin.

"Of course you're right, dear." She smiled and gave Kate an obvious wink.

"Yeah," Robert said, "I know you two. But seriously, you eat this. I have to go make some business calls from the motel room."

Their mother frowned. "That motel must be costing you a fortune."

"No, it's reasonable," he said. "Kate can stay for a week or two and I'll drive back and forth from home. If you think this food is bad, you should see the meals in that motel restaurant." He got up to go, flashing Kate a glance of collusion. "I'll be back after supper."

His footsteps echoed down the hallway. Kate and her mother looked wordlessly at each other, relieved. Kate looked away guiltily. Then her mother spoke, apologetic. "He's so tired," she said. "He's been with me since yesterday."

She looked at Kate, then into the air of the room. "I'm in a fix," she said. "Except for when the pain comes, it's all a show that goes on without me. I'm like an invalid, or a lunatic."

Kate moved close and touched her mother's arms. "That's all right, we're going to get you through it. Someone's covering for you at work?"

"I had to take a leave of absence. It's going to take a while afterward—"

"I know. But it's the last thing to worry about, it can't be helped."

"Like spilt milk. Isn't that what they say?"

"I don't know what they say. But why didn't you tell me? Didn't you know something was wrong?"

"Yes . . . bad headaches. Migraines, I thought, or the diabetes getting worse. I was afraid they'd start me on insulin." She tightened the corner of her mouth. "Little did I know . . ."

They heard the shuffle of slippers. An old woman stood at the open door of the room, looking in confusedly. She seemed about to speak, then moved on.

"Oh," said Kate's mother in exasperation, "shut that door, please? They let these old women wander around like refugees." She sat up, reaching for a robe. "And let's get me out of this bed."

They sat near the window while she finished eating. Bars of moted yellow banded the floor of the room. The light held a tinge of spring which seemed painful because it might vanish. They heard the rattle of the meal cart outside the closed door, and the clunk-slide of patients with aluminum walkers. Kate's mother sighed and pushed away the half-empty soup bowl.

"They'll be here after me any minute. More tests. I just want to stay with you." Her face was warm and smooth in the slanted light, lines in her skin delicate, unreal; as though a face behind her face was now apparent after many years. She sat looking at Kate and smiled.

"One day when you were about four you were dragging a broom around the kitchen. I asked what you were doing and you told me that when you got old you were going to be an angel and sweep the rotten rain off the clouds."

"What did you say to that?"

"I said that when you were old I was sure God would see to

it." Her mother laughed. "I'm glad you weren't such a smart aleck then," she said. "You would have told me my view of God was paternalistic."

"Ah yes," sighed Kate. "God, that famous dude. Here I am, getting old, facing unemployment, alone, and where is He?"

"You're not alone," her mother said, "I'm right here."

Kate didn't answer. She sat motionless and felt her heart begin to open like a box with a hinged lid. The fullness had no edges.

Her mother stood. She rubbed her hands slowly, twisting her wedding rings. "My hands are so dry in the winter," she said softly, "I brought some hand cream with me but I can't find it anywhere, my suitcase is so jumbled. Thank heavens spring is early this year. . . . They told me that little park over there doesn't usually open till the end of March . . ."

She's helping me, thought Kate, I'm not supposed to let her down.

". . . but they're already running it on weekends. Even past dusk. We'll see the lights tonight. You can't see the shapes this far away, just the motion . . ."

A nurse came in with a wheelchair. Kate's mother pulled a wry face. "This wheelchair is a bit much," she said.

"We don't want to tire you out," said the nurse.

The chair took her weight quietly. At the door she put out her hand to stop, turned, and said anxiously, "Kate, see if you can find that hand cream?"

It was the blue suitcase from years ago, still almost new. She'd brought things she never used for everyday; a cashmere sweater, lace slips, silk underpants wrapped in tissue. Folded beneath was a stack of postmarked envelopes, slightly ragged,

tied with twine. Kate opened one and realized that all the cards
were there, beginning with the first of the marriage. There
were a few photographs of her and Robert, baby pictures almost
indistinguishable from each other, and then Kate's homemade
Valentines, fastened together with rubber bands. Kate stared.
What will I do with these things? She wanted air; she needed to
breathe. She walked to the window and put the bundled papers
on the sill. She'd raised the glass and pushed back the screen
when suddenly, her mother's clock radio went off with a flat
buzz. Kate moved to switch it off and brushed the cards with
her arm. Envelopes shifted and slid, scattering on the floor of
the room. A few snapshots wafted silently out the window. They
dipped and turned, twirling. Kate didn't try to reach them.
They seemed only scraps, buoyant and yellowed, blown away,
the faces small as pennies. Somewhere far-off there were sirens,
almost musical, drawn out and carefully approaching.

The nurse came in with evening medication. Kate's mother
lay in bed. "I hope this is strong enough," she said. "Last night
I couldn't sleep at all. So many sounds in a hospital . . ."

"You'll sleep tonight," the nurse assured her.

Kate winked at her mother. "That's right," she said, "I'll help
you out if I have to."

They stayed up for an hour, watching the moving lights outside and the stationary glows of houses across the distant river.
The halls grew darker, were lit with night lights, and the hospital dimmed. Kate waited. Her mother's eyes fluttered and finally she slept. Her breathing was low and regular.

Kate didn't move. Robert had said he'd be back; where was
he? She felt a sunken anger and shook her head. She'd been on
the point of telling her mother everything. The secrets were a

travesty. What if there were things her mother wanted done, people she needed to see? Kate wanted to wake her before these hours passed in the dark and confess that she had lied. Between them, through the tension, there had always been a trusted clarity. Now it was twisted. Kate sat leaning forward, nearly touching the hospital bed.

Suddenly her mother sat bolt upright, her eyes open and her face transfixed. She looked blindly toward Kate but seemed to see nothing. "Who are you?" she whispered. Kate stood, at first unable to move. The woman in the bed opened and closed her mouth several times, as though she were gasping. Then she said loudly, "Stop moving the table. Stop it this instant!" Her eyes were wide with fright and her body was vibrating.

Kate reached her. "Mama, wake up, you're dreaming." Her mother jerked, flinging her arms out. Kate held her tightly.

"I can hear the wheels," she moaned.

"No, no," Kate said. "You're here with me."

"It's not so?"

"No," Kate said. "It's not so."

She went limp. Kate felt for her pulse and found it rapid, then regular. She sat rocking her mother. In a few minutes she lay her back on the pillows and smoothed the damp hair at her temples, smoothed the sheets of the bed. Later she slept fitfully in a chair, waking repeatedly to assure herself that her mother was breathing.

Near dawn she got up, exhausted, and left the room to walk in the corridor. In front of the window at the end of the hallway she saw a man slumped on a couch; the man slowly stood and wavered before her like a specter. It was Robert.

"Kate?" he said.

Years ago he had flunked out of a small junior college and their mother sat in her bedroom rocker, crying hard for over an hour while Kate tried in vain to comfort her. Kate went to the

university the next fall, so anxious that she studied frantically,
outlining whole textbooks in yellow ink. She sat in the front
rows of large classrooms to take voluminous notes, writing
quickly in her thick notebook. Robert had gone home, held a
job in a plant that manufactured business forms and worked his
way through the hometown college. By that time their father
was dead, and Robert became, always and forever, the man of
the house.

"Robert," Kate said, "I'll stay. Go home."

After breakfast they sat waiting for Robert, who had called
and said he'd arrive soon. Kate's fatigue had given way to an in
tense awareness of every sound, every gesture. How would
they get through the day? Her mother had awakened from the
drugged sleep still groggy, unable to eat. The meal was sent
away untouched and she watched the window as though she
feared the walls of the room.

"I'm glad your father isn't here to see this," she said. There
was a silence and Kate opened her mouth to speak. "I mean,"
said her mother quickly, "I'm going to look horrible for a few
weeks, with my head all shaved." She pulled an afghan up
around her lap and straightened the magazines on the table be
side her chair.

"Mom," Kate said, "your hair will grow back."

Her mother pulled the afghan closer. "I've been thinking of
your father," she said. "It's not that I'd have wanted him to suf
fer. But if he had to die, sometimes I wish he'd done it more
gently. That heart attack, so finished; never a warning. I wish
I'd had some time to nurse him. In a way, it's a chance to settle
things."

"Did things need settling?"

"They always do, don't they?" She sat looking out the window, then said softly, "I wonder where I'm headed."

"You're not headed anywhere," Kate said. "I want you right here to see me settle down into normal American womanhood."

Her mother smiled reassuringly. "Where are my grandchildren?" she said. "That's what I'd like to know."

"You stick around," said Kate, "and I promise to start working on it." She moved her chair closer, so that their knees were touching and they could both see out the window. Below them cars moved on the highway and the Ferris wheel in the little park was turning.

"I remember when you were one of the little girls in the parade at the county fair. You weren't even in school yet; you were beautiful in that white organdy dress and pinafore. You wore those shiny black patent shoes and a crown of real apple blossoms. Do you remember?"

"Yes," Kate said. "That long parade. They told me not to move and I sat so still my legs went to sleep. When they lifted me off the float I couldn't stand up. They put me under a tree to wait for you, and you came, in a full white skirt and white sandals, your hair tied back in a red scarf. I can see you yet."

Her mother laughed. "Sounds like a pretty exaggerated picture."

Kate nodded. "I was little. You were big."

"You loved the county fair. You were wild about the carnivals." They looked down at the little park. "Magic, isn't it?" her mother said.

"Maybe we could go see it," said Kate. "I'll ask the doctor."

They walked across a pedestrian footbridge spanning the highway. Kate had bundled her mother into a winter coat and gloves despite the sunny weather. The day was sharp, nearly still, holding its bright air like illusion. Kate tasted the brittle water of her breath, felt for the cool handrail and thin steel o the webbed fencing. Cars moved steadily under the bridge. Beyond a muted roar of motors the park spread green and wooded, its limits clearly visible.

Kate's mother had combed her hair and put on lipstick. Her mouth was defined and brilliant; she linked arms with Kate like an escort. "I was afraid they'd tell us no," she said. "I was ready to run away!"

"I promised I wouldn't let you. And we only have ten min utes, long enough for the Ferris wheel." Kate grinned.

"I haven't ridden one in years. I wonder if I still know how."

"Of course you do. Ferris wheels are genetic knowledge."

"All right, whatever you say." She smiled. "We'll just hold on."

They drew closer and walked quickly through the sounds o the highway. When they reached the grass it was ankle-high and thick, longer and more ragged than it appeared from a dis tance. The Ferris wheel sat squarely near a grove of swaying elms, squat and laboring, taller than trees. Its neon lights still burned, pale in the sun, spiraling from inside like an imagined bloom. The naked elms surrounded it, their topmost branches tapping. Steel ribs of the machine were graceful and slightly rusted, squeaking faintly above a tinkling music. Only a few people were riding.

"Looks a little rickety," Kate said.

"Oh, don't worry," said her mother.

Kate tried to buy tickets but the ride was free. The old man running the motor wore an engineer's cap and patched overalls. He stopped the wheel and led them on a short ramp to an open car. It dipped gently, padded with black cushions. An orderly and his children rode in the car above. Kate saw their dangling feet, the girls' dusty sandals and gray socks beside their father's shoes and the hem of his white pants. The youngest one swung her feet absently, so it seemed the breeze blew her legs like fabric hung on a line.

Kate looked at her mother. "Are you ready for the big sky?" They laughed. Beyond them the river moved lazily. Houses on the opposite bank seemed empty, but a few rowboats bobbed at the docks. The surface of the water lapped and reflected clouds, and as Kate watched, searching for a definition of line, the Ferris wheel jerked into motion. The car rocked. They looked into the distance and Kate caught her mother's hand as they ascended.

Far away the hospital rose up white and glistening, its windows catching the glint of the sun. Directly below, the park was nearly deserted. There were a few cars in the parking lot and several dogs chasing each other across the grass. Two or three lone women held children on the teeter-totters and a wind was coming up. The forlorn swings moved on their chains. Kate had a vision of the park at night, totally empty, wind weaving heavily through the trees and children's playthings like a great black fish about to surface. She felt a chill on her arms. The light had gone darker, quietly, like a minor chord.

"Mom," Kate said, "it's going to storm." Her own voice seemed distant, the sound strained through layers of screen or gauze.

"No," said her mother, "it's going to pass over." She moved her hand to Kate's knee and touched the cloth of her daughter's skirt.

Kate gripped the metal bar at their waists and looked straight ahead. They were rising again and she felt she would scream. She tried to breathe rhythmically, steadily. She felt the immense weight of the air as they moved through it.

They came almost to the top and stopped. The little car swayed back and forth.

"You're sick, aren't you," her mother said.

Kate shook her head. Below them the grass seemed to glitter coldly, like a sea. Kate sat wordless, feeling the touch of her mother's hand. The hand moved away and Kate felt the absence of the warmth.

They looked at each other levelly.

"I know all about it," her mother said, "I know what you haven't told me."

The sky circled around them, a sure gray movement. Kate swallowed calmly and let their gaze grow endless. She saw herself in her mother's wide brown eyes and felt she was falling slowly into them.

What It Takes to Keep a Young Girl Alive

She signed her name and the recruiter told her to be there May 5th, everyone would have a lot of fun. Maple Point was trying to outdo Disneyland and Sue was trying to leave home. They hired boys to cook and girls to serve food and run rides. Courtesy Corps girls were blonds in yellow suits and white gloves and broadbrim hats. They stood under white umbrellas and answered questions but Sue was a waitress at the Silver Nickel. Where everything was striped and a fake piano tinkled. Girls from Tennessee had rimmed eyes and hot skins. They had to wait on everyone within four minutes while the managers walked around saying Pick up that crust. The boys in the kitchen kept a list of everyone who cried. At the end of the summer they bought a present for the girl who had cried the

most. Sue felt their white judgment on her like a sun lightin
up the pale thick hair on her arms. A customer found a fl
under his egg and the manager accused her of carelessness. Su
said the fly must have been on the plate in the kitchen, since
couldn't have picked up the egg and crawled under it. But
was her responsibility to check the plates.

Sue lived in a three-story army barracks. Each room had a
iron bunk on one wall, a single cot on the other, and a dresse
in the aisle. They stood on their beds to dress. A red storn
fence around the perimeter was strung with barbed wire to pro
tect everyone. Each morning the walks were littered with in
sects swarmed in sick off Lake Erie. One day they carried a gi
out of the barracks wrapped in an army blanket. They found he
in the showers. Sue saw her rounded buttocks sag the oliv
wool. Inside there she was sticky. They said she was from Siou
City. Birthmark on her face with tiny dents like a seeded straw
berry. Sue had seen her running the dime movies in the Penn
Arcade, Theda Bara with a gold fan and shadow eyes.

Sue got off work and drifted down the midway in a wet heat
past the American-flag petunia gardens. Screamers rammed cir
cles in the Whirl-A-Gig cars, pasted in stand-up Roll-A-Tur
cages by their own gravity. They whistled and moved in drove
behind raw hot dogs. At night she lay in the top bunk nake
with the lights off. Fan on full aimed at her crotch while janitor
lounged in front of the garages watching the rows of windows
Rod Stewart, scratchy and loud, combed his hair in a thousan
ways and came out looking just the same.

Cheers

The sewing woman lived across the tracks, down past Arey's Feed Store. Row of skinny houses on a mud alley. Her rooms smelled of salted grease and old newspaper. Behind the ironing board she was thin, scooping up papers that shuffled open in her hands. Her eyebrows were arched sharp and painted on.

She made cheerleading suits for ten-year-olds. Threading the machine, she clicked her red nails on the needle and pulled my shirt over my head. In the other room the kids watched *Queen for a Day*. She bent over me. I saw each eyelash painted black and hard and separate. Honey, she said. Turn around this way. And on the wall there was a postcard of orange trees in Florida. A man in a straw hat reached up with his hand all curled. Beautiful Bounty said the card in wavy red letters.

I got part of it made up, she said, fitting the red vest. You girls are bout the same size as mine All you girls are bout the same. She pursed her red lips and pinched the cloth together. Tell me somethin Honey. How'd I manage all these kids an no man. On television there was loud applause for the queen, whose roses were sharp and real. Her machine buzzed like an animal beside the round clock. She frowned as she pressed the button with her foot, then furled the red cloth out and pulled me to her. Her pointed white face was smudged around the eyes. I watched the pale strand of scalp in her hair. There, she said.

When I left she tucked the money in her sweater. She had pins between her teeth and lipstick gone grainy in the cracks of her mouth. I had a red swing skirt and a bumpy A on my chest. Lord, she said. You do look pretty.

Snow

The school opened iron gates to show its clowns and jugglers. Crowds came to watch the mutes, the senseless ones. Those lawns and high walls were not so fearsome in summer, and flags rippled from posts striped with crepe paper by the deaf. Molly's father stood beside her holding Callie. Molly watched Laura; Laura was her mother. The crowd pressed up and Laura danced, with her light hair blowing wild about her face and the filmy dress moving to show her legs. The focus of her blind eyes didn't change even in leaping; in those controlled jumps which could not keep her arms from rising, as though the feeling of air made her want to enter it. Afterward she stood very still. The dress blew about her thighs. Men in the back of the crowd began to hoot. But the rain came on. A wind blew up and knocked over one of the stands. The flimsy stand broke and let fly two hundred balloons; people scrambled and fell on each other to catch them. Molly saw the colors twisting. Her father stood beside her but he could not see, ever. Laura stood there listening. And the balloons went up.

The town slept and remembered wars. Especially in heat, it slept. The river shrunk in its deep bed; clay along the dried banks grew giant cracks. Every day was very long and it was 1948. Molly thought it would always be this way. Spenser, South Carolina, had two factories, a lumber mill and a training parlor for beauticians. There were three grade schools, a grammar school, a high school and a business college. And there was the School for the Deaf, Dumb and Blind where Molly's father taught. Everywhere there were heavy trees hung with ivy that threw their long shadows out even on the hottest days. Molly and her mother took Callie to the park. In summer they bought sno-cones from a man with one eye and a red-striped coat. His name was Barney and Molly asked him where his eye was.

My eye? he said. Wouldn't surprise me none if somebody had my eye in a box this minute.

He laughed loudly. Molly knew he could see. His one eye wasn't still like her mother's eyes, but darted back and forth like the head of a quirky bird. Molly was only glad nobody had her mother's eyes in a box, but was suddenly afraid and clutched at her.

Mr. Parsons, Laura said. You've frightened her.

But he had seen it already with his one eye and was bending over Molly. Why Honey, he said. Don't you worry. Ain't nobody going to touch them jewels of your Mama's. Why if they got close, their hands would turn to ice like this here.

And Molly watched him dip the crushed white into paper

cones with painted clowns and balloons on them like at the fair.
Then he poured blue syrup over for blueberry and red for
strawberry. Callie was sitting in his stroller watching with his
big eyes that caught and held but were focused far away like
Mama's. He watched Barney hold the long colored bottle up
high and squirt the bright blue far down as it faded into the ice.
Molly watched the color go. Her mother's eyes were pale like
ice, that cool blue smoke of hard ice. Barney would give them
the cones and they'd go over on the grass and eat them, Callie
falling and pushing his fat hands. The paper cones got melty and
the balloons would bleed.

Molly asked her mother, These clowns can't hear what we
say, can they?

She said, Molly, all clowns aren't deaf.

They'd walk back later, having stayed by the duck pond for
hours because Callie loved to be near the water. Laura would
walk down to the edge of the pond. She made a sound so much
like the low murmurings of the ducks that they'd get confused
and swim close. Callie would sit absolutely still. Molly put him
in the stroller to leave and he'd turn his head to hear the ducks
until she'd pushed him to the top of the hill. Molly told him the
ducks were still there, they were always there. Her mother's
stick reached out in front, thin whisk back and forth. Laura felt
for the curbs and stones and she pushed the stroller one-
handed. Molly walked holding to the other side. Near dusk; how
the heavy dark-leaved trees hung over them and the stroller's
wheels creaked uneven on brick sidewalks up Spenser Hill.
They would talk, walking till they got to the house. Molly knew
her father had lemonade in the tall glass pitcher on the blue
table. Her mother would say, Randal, you're home so soon? and
he'd answer, No, Laura, you're late. Oh Randal, not again, and
she would touch him like she did, her pale hands behind his
head.

Once when they were downtown, Laura spoke to Molly and she didn't answer. Standing by the stroller as always, Molly didn't answer and waited to see what would happen. Laura felt with her hand but Molly knelt below it, hearing the edge in her mother's voice and ashamed now but afraid. Laura said, Molly? in different directions and screamed finally, Molly! Albers, from the bookstore, was behind them.

He said to her quietly, Mrs. Collier, here's Molly.

Molly, don't joke with me, she said. And as soon as he had passed, she leaned close, murmuring. But it wasn't a joke, was it.

At night Molly's father came to talk to her. Callie was asleep in the other bed, his thumb jammed in his mouth. Muted light from the streetlamp swam through the windows. She could see the tiny frenzied swarming of insects in ellipses around the yellow globe. Light fell blue on Callie's face; his cheeks were gone in the shadows. That night all her father said to her was, Molly, no one can always take care of you.

Then he told the story of the dancing princess who lifted up her bed at night to go down the silver steps.

But what did she do down there?

She danced, he said, like your mother at the fair. And wore out all her slippers.

Up and down the block they heard footsteps on the sidewalks. Still it was not night. Doors shut their private sounds. Cars purred a muffled chugging as they slowed for the turn, then growled deep as they picked up speed. Her father told the story all the way through, and by the end Molly wasn't listening anymore; only watched his big shape and his hands in the air that fell and stayed in her hair. His lips moved in his still face, and the dark came.

* * *

Molly, Molly, he thought as she sank in her rocking sleep.
He was himself a light sleeper, waking from dreams several
times a night to hear the house settle around him. It made him
wonder that his daughter should draw shut like Lazarus, and no
sound would wake her until she swam up alone from where she
had been. He wondered how she dreamed. He sat on her bed
with his hand in her hair trying to hear her dreams.

When Randal first began teaching Braille, the young wife of
one of his students asked him how a blind person dreams. Randal told her that the sounds and voices have their own shapes
and varied thicknesses. Almost like colors, infinite shades of silver. Randal realized then that his sight in dreams was that of his
childhood; blurred moving shapes with a light or emptiness
behind them. In dreams he could still almost see the fingers on
a hand, the beautiful separated films that moved differently and
by themselves.

When he was seven he'd had measles and diptheria. His
burning eyes were bandaged. He saw nothing. He practiced
remembering how the fingers looked, how they moved in and
out and touched and laced their translucence into a ball. When
he bandages came away, it was all black. Slowly there was
lighter gray, and lighter. In a year he could watch the glimmered blur of bodies running (the violent smacking bat, boys'
voices in sweet rising fold Get him out! Get him out! feet
thudding close and gone), but not again the lovely fingers. The
lovely—

Randal? Laura's quiet voice was by the door. What are you
doing in there so long?

I thought you were asleep, he said. He knew she saw no
shapes. Just the black. When they married, her aunt in Wash-

ington said now she would never get well (Married to a blind
man my God. I did what I could she wants to ruin her life
wash my hands of it).

You know I can't sleep until you come to bed, said Laura.
She heard sadness in his voice, more slow distance than pain, as
if he struggled patiently in a closet. She never questioned his
sadness. She heard his broad hands smooth Molly's bedclothes
and then the lifting of his weight as the bed shifted its layers.

He straightened and walked to her. She leaned against him
heavily, felt him solid under the robe. Smelling him, she
pressed her face where the cloth opened on his chest; touched
her mouth to the skin and the fine hair. When she was sixteen
he had taught her to read with her fingers and make love. He
had given something up to her and she kept it for him.

I've made some tea, it'll help you sleep, she said. Did you
talk to Molly?

I didn't, much. I don't think she'll do it again.

Randal felt Laura's small hard shoulders. It seemed to him
that she was made of light, that she would float out of his heavi-
ness on the earth, in this town and this house. He felt her pull
away.

I forgot the spoons, she said. She went to the kitchen. He
heard her long thin feet on the bare floor, the opening
drawers, the inanimate silver talking its clatter. In their room
the windows were open. The lace curtains dipped in and out
catching on the rosebushes. She had turned down the bed on
his side. He knew she had lain there beside the neat triangle of
sheet, waiting for him.

Randal, she said, did I tell you they're building a merry-go-
round in the park? With a calliope and horses ordered from
New York. Mr. Parsons told us about it. Won't Molly love it.

Laura handed him the steaming cup and her hand brushing
his was cool next to the heat.

When she was sleeping and he woke at night, there was
nothing. There was the house aching. There was the street and
the plants moving by the window. At night the magnolias
drifted their fleshy scent; he lay and sweat. He felt his son sleep
blond and floating in another room that was gone that was oh far
gone. His son drifted, a son asleep, born in a worsening
trouble. He heard Molly weeping into her hands, Molly a
grown woman and her heavy black hair in her face. He pulled
Laura close to him and her scent washed over him like slow
water. He held her sleeping body and was alone until the panic
passed.

It was raining. He gradually heard and lay listening (his feet
on cold steps and the milk wagon creaking, early morning,
wheel's groan, hooves on wet stones and yes the musky steaming smell, Randal get back inside You'll catch your death No
you can't touch, but he pulled and ran, the man bundled him,
lifted him, And the horse, big, its long hard velvet head). Laura
moved breathless and naked to shut the windows.

The curtains are soaked, she said, I didn't hear it raining.

She stood by the window in the watery air, smelling the
warm asphalt cool. When she was a child she had seen rain. She
remembered it fell in a slanted color. Pearls and ash falling.
Rain came from far off to contain everything. You could see it
coming. It rained those weeks in the hospital when they
operated on her head. They said it was the tail end of a hurri-
cane, named for her because she was the littlest girl on the
ward (I'm not little I'm eight and I can read *Ivanhoe*. No one
said anything. She knew she couldn't read it anymore). Later
they asked her to remember. Remember all about it; her
mother, the man, the car. Nothing there. For six years, Laura
sat in her aunt's house. A sequence of paid widows read aloud
to her. Her aunt read the Old Testament.

Your mother, she said, was my sister born in innocence and

consumed by her own soul. You are the innocent fruit of her repetitious sin. As we sow, so shall we reap.

Laura sewed; rapidly, constantly, perfectly: long afternoons by a window open even in winter. Unconscious of her finger's penance on a raised design in linen, she heard and smelled the street. When Laura was fourteen, her aunt became afraid of her. She ordered that Laura's hair be cut; she sent her to the school. In two years, Randal came.

Randal heard Laura's fingers stroke the polished windowsill. Rain continued, round. Those years ago her belly was globed and tight with a hollow floating. He remembered the long night of first labor . . . long, long. How she held her breath and spent it, blowing air like an animal adapted to ocean. Then it was over; he heard her fingers on the baby's face. Raining on the sheathed head, first memorizing, then just looking again and again. And he touched her forehead, which always had a peculiar heat to it when she was happy.

When Callie's nose bled, the rocking chairs got blurry. Their shiny arms rippled and ran over themselves. He was five. They bought him glasses and Molly went to school. Molly went to school, putting her face in front of him where she knew he could see, saying Callie, Callie, don't untie the string. She had told him about the string no one could see. She said it kept his feet on the ground. She rubbed his back with her hand and took her book away.

You can't read, she said. It's not good for you.

And the door opened. All the cool rained air came in. He heard her feet on the sidewalk; he heard her brown shoes with their neat ties on the crisscrossed brick that was washed now. Fat dark worms writhed on the cool grit. His father said they were trying to find dirt when they rolled like that. He said they were drowning in the air.

Callie heard the cat scratching at the window and dimly saw it beyond the glass. It opened its mouth soundlessly wide and to Callie it looked like a pink hole opening in a steam. Things seemed closer than they were; things were there before he touched them. He pushed his hands through the veil that surrounded them. Then there was a hardness.

They took him to the special doctor's and he read the pictures. There was a boat, and then two boats, and then two cowboys and a boat in the shape of a triangle. He couldn't see the cowboys' faces anymore, but he remembered what they looked like from before. He told how they looked. They were the same one two times, with their big eyes rolled to the side and their smiles and their hats. They looked like they were turning and something pressed them flat. He thought they were afraid of the boat coming. When he squinted he could make the boat roll over them. Then he pulled it back and they were still turning.

He could read the chart with the letters on it. But Molly said not to tell, and now she wouldn't let him read her books. With his glasses on he could see the big letters again. He never took the glasses off. He tried to sleep with them on. Each night his father's big hand came down and took them in the dark. The hand was big and dark and his father sang to him when he took the glasses.

I wish I was an apple. A hangin in a tree.

His father sang it very slowly, trembling his voice. The apple was in the tree. It was round and red and it had a heart. It was made of sugar. When he got to the part about the girl, his father's voice went up and around and in; still slower, like a heavy animal moving in a snow. Callie had heard about snow.

And every time my Sweetheart passed she'd. Take a bite of me.

Now it was snowing and he and his father walked with the girl to get along home. Callie led them all home because he could see. The girl was his mother but she was not his mother. She was Cindy; Callie knew that, but the song smelled of his mother.

Get along home. Get along. Home.

His father's voice was slower, slow and high. There was cold honey in the snow.

Get along. Home Cindy Cindy. I'll marry you suh uhm. Time.

Apples were fallen in the snow and the honey. They went along home until they were gone.

Callie and his mother went to the movies. Molly went to school. She saw the movies on Saturdays, but not on Wednesdays. When he and his mother went. They walked down the hill on the skinny sidewalk. He held her hand and her stick tapped out in front. It tapped very lightly like the thin finger of a clock. Sometimes he heard it tapping when his mother was asleep, tapping from the dark corner of the room. He heard all the clocks tapping in the velvet house. He knew the stick told them when to tap.

As they walked, his mother asked him to look up in the sky and tell her what creatures were there. A creature was like an animal but it could be people, or half girl and half horse. Creatures grew in the sky, sliding over each other. Once a cloud came down and covered the town. His mother said it was a creature of a sort, a fog; only he couldn't see its shape because he was inside it. She said she had seen many creatures when she was a girl. The best one was a man with a big pocket in his vest. More creatures kept coming out of the pocket until the man himself came out and then there was nothing left.

There were two movie theaters in town. The finer one was actually closer. But his mother liked the smaller one that was on

lown Main Street close to the tracks. It was nearly empty in the
afternoons except for them and the sweeping man, who moved
his big flat broom around and around. The lobby floor was laid
with yellow linoleum in diamond shapes. It was coming up in
patches where the planked boards showed through black with
fuzz. Trains went by and the big mirrors rattled on the walls. In
the shadowy closeness their seats shook; he gripped the worn
plush delirious with joy.

The screen was a floating square of light. Curtains swung
back on rods. His mother cupped his face in the dark. Pouring
out of a tiny hole the big lion opened and roared, shuddering its
gold weight. With his glasses Callie could almost see the tiny
eyes and the fragile underlip quivering its teeth.

On the screen a man danced with a hat rack, holding it like
some tender thing and twirling it over his back. He danced his
feet around while it circled like a saucer on its side. Tippling its
fluted legs, tippling it turned a long brown liquid in his arms in
his thin arms. His shiny heels clicked and spun, his mouth a
perfect kiss. He was supple and dapper and his smooth face
rippled in the shaking of the trains. Callie was not afraid in the
dark because the man was dancing. He danced over the rumble
of the blunt-nosed engine and the clack of the boxcar wheels.
He danced the tiled cement in front of the old theater and the
steamy sidewalk grate. He danced the long cracked Spenser
streets under the droop-haired trees, up the hill to the house
where Callie's father sat with clinched hands, listening to Cho-
pin in the dark. Callie dreamed them together in the dark
house; his mother in the thin hallway, her white dress, her legs
clear through the cloth. His father sitting with his music by the
rainy window and they were all safe with the dancing man.

It went black and the lights came up. Callie waited for his
mother to know, and they walked up the slanted floor to the
lobby. It looked smaller to him now, gauzy as a cataract. Night,

said the sweeping man. His broom went round and round. They
pushed open the double doors and the soft fatal whish of his
moving followed them away.

Laura put Callie down to sleep when they got home. She
wondered why sleep is down. She thought it was like a sinking.
Callie was afraid to sleep. She sat by him until he slept and put
his glasses where he could reach them.

She pressed herself against the straight back of the wooden
chair and touched her face with her hands. She felt the round
covered balls of her eyes, the boned sockets, the hard line of
her jaw. Her face felt old to her when she touched it; when she
was alone and touched it. She hadn't seen her face since she
was a child. She remembered seeing it that night in the mirror;
the hall light a sudden blindness, her mother laughing, the
sweet sick smell as she leaned close to tie a red ribbon too loose
in Laura's hair. It fell lopsided in her light hair, in the mirror.
She saw her own eyes, then her mother looking at her. And the
man laughed, holding them both, and the car was warm, moving. She crawled into the back and rolled against the seat. They
laughed, her mother dangling the discarded ribbon from the
rearview mirror, the wrinkled raveled satin, and the car lurched
and they laughed.

Laura's head was aching. She would not think of it. She
would go and lay in the snow. Behind her mother's house the
snow was deep. Laura move your arms up and down like this.
And your legs, there, like this . . . Laura would close her eyes
under the pines in her warm clothes, feel snow falling on her
face . . . all sounds went away. And her mother lifted her
laughing Silly don't fall asleep in the snow . . .

Laura got up and walked through the quiet house to the bedroom. Clocks ticked. She took off her clothes and folded them neatly across a chair. A car went by. She thought it must be dark by now. She was very tired. She got between the covers, feeling the wide empty bed with her legs. It seemed to open, the sheets opening and covering. In the snow they lay down to make women in gowns whose arms had exploded. No Laura, those are angels with wings like the angel in the tree . . . Snow fell from the trees in clumps, filled the angels up. Laura stamped the exploded arms. Again, in her dreams, she saw the shadow with the open mouth, falling all in fire. It had the sweet sick smell of her mother's words; it crooned, falling the crackling black. Good black and the words said hush. Laura slept. She was sinking and the sounds went away.

On Wednesdays Randal took Molly to the diner. It was a long aluminum room with yellow stools and a red counter. Ralph was a man near fifty whose rubbery face ran with sweat. He shook Molly's hand and called her a lady. Randal and Molly sat up front near the grill. Behind the counter Ralph's flaccid daughter Sylvie smiled her sideways smile and nodded her head again and again.

Ralph made a bowl of batter for their pancakes. Sylvie shambled blond and big, reaching under the counter for the silverware. How you, she nodded, placing each utensil carefully beside the other. When he heard her turn to get the water glasses, Randal turned the silverware right side up. Molly watched Sylvie put three ice cubes in each glass, one at a time, with her big silver dipper. She put the glasses in front of them and smiled, her mouth twitching. Her father liked the blind man and told her to wait on him good. Her eyes rolled to the door, swept the wall and the square clock, swept it all to the far end of the red counter. Her hand moved on her thigh as if she held the rag that wiped the Formica clean. Her hands smelled like the rag. Its wilted pungence mixed with an oily peanut smell when she lifted her arms.

Her baby, Howard, was on the floor like always, playing with straws or spoons. He was a fat towheaded baby who never cried. Sylvie picked him up and held him on her lap while Randal and Molly ate pancakes. Uh huh, huh, Sylvie laughed slow, the baby rocking. Randal thought: she is like a cow burning. He asked her how the week had been, feeling Molly watch her.

Ralph scraped the grill with his iron spatula. Welfare people been to see my girl again, he said, but she can count to twenty now. She ain't the first one been taken advantage of—Look here, Mr. Collier, I got new berries and cream for them pancakes.

The syrup was warm in Randal's mouth. Molly's fingers curled on his wrist were sticky, her small nails sharp. Her stolid hands weren't Laura's. Laura's hands (the school that first month, his quarters a room in the tower; savage thumps of pigeons on the ledge. The psychiatrist crossed and recrossed his legs. Laura is a special case Her blindness, he said, Is to some extent hysterical . . . thrown free, the car . . . her mother crawled out burning, he said. We think Laura was, he said, Conscious. Gloves at night for years, he said, To keep from hurting . . . herself in her sleep. I'm not qualified, he said, To deal with her).

Later, Laura gave Randal the gloves. They were white cotton gloves like young girls wear to church; but they knotted around the wrists with string. Her hands, thought Randal. Sylvie went on with her sounds.

Laura came to his rooms on the grounds. He hadn't been near her for several weeks. I'm seventeen, she'd said, today I'm seventeen. She came near him, pulling at his hands his chest his hair. He was afraid her aunt would find out and take her away (She's a slut like her mother. You're not the first or last. I did what I could now she's your affair). He lived in fear she would be gone or pregnant too soon; still he wanted her so badly he shook. By the time her pregnancy showed, she was eighteen and they were married. Randal was thirty-eight, moving in her arms in their empty house. On the blond wood floors she taught him to waltz. They turned, turning until he was dizzy and he pressed her to him and they lay down on the floor she—

Take your time, said Ralph. Just sweeping up. Randal reached in his pocket for the money.

Outside, the diner's purple lights made the wet street pink. The door clicked behind them and did its slow sigh shut. Molly listened. Sylvie pushed her ragged mop and chanted. Nine, ten, eleven.

Callie heard them come in. His father scuffed his feet and then they were in the room. They all went out to the kitchen. His mother had soup for them and the steam came up. His father's face above him was wide and lost in the steam. Callie reached through and touched him and left his hand there.

When Callie was in the white room, his father's face had been too wide and frightened him. Then he couldn't pull the light on by himself and the woman with the cool hands picked him up to put him in the bed. Things were different before he went to the white room; a face sat on top of a face and blurred where they came together. There were angles of light and two prismed doors in the wall. There were two of everything. Nothing was ever by itself because everything faded its edges into something else. Callie was lonely when he saw that his mother had only one face. She had seemed to be all around him. Her arms legs hips breasts hands hair had been in his sight a milky atmosphere. Now he saw that everyone was separate.

Callie ate his soup. Their separate faces moved around him in the steam. They receded, each one behind a single veil. Their voices shimmered behind the colors and broke.

Callie's mother broke eggs. She held one in the curve of her hand and clicked it against the bowl. She felt for the crack and she pulled it apart; there was a suck of air to break your heart.

No, Callie, she said. That's cracks in the sidewalk, to break your back. But you can say it anyway you want to, especially on your birthday.

She gave him an egg to break. It sat in his hand all round and full. No eyes no ears no arms, it was a poor thing. He wanted to keep it.

No, his mother said. It's for your cake. But he ran away with it and put it in a box.

They had a party. They sang the birthday song and it had the same words over and over. They sang it again and again, so slow to the burning candles. Callie blew them to sleep. He walked his fingers around them and made marks in the icing like tiny feet. There was a fire engine in the bag. It screamed when it ran. Callie hated it crying. His father did something to it and then it ran quietly, whispering its wheels. His mother gave him a small gold circle hung with slender pipes. She said they were chimes and they talked in the dark. She hung them in his window and brushed his eyes with her mouth.

Then it was night. They left him alone in his bed. From nowhere there was a sound that flew; the tiny pipes sang when they touched. The fire engine stayed very still. Callie held the egg in his hand. He moved it; he felt something twirl inside the shell.

* * *

Molly's father said his own rhymes to Callie and her:

> Molly Molly Pumpkin Polly
> How does your garden growl
> With seahorse bells and turtle shells
> And midget men all in the aisle

Somewhere, she thought, little men held sea horses in their
arms like dogs; seahorses with bells inside them like the bells in
the clock on the wall. In that place, the wind left all the hours
growling in the grass, soft and scared like Sylvie's repetitive
laugh. Molly asked her father where the garden was. He said he
would try to remember, but when you try to find some things,
there is a snow comes down.

Once it snowed in Spenser. Callie was six but he never went
to school. Their father carried him out to see the snow. Molly
looked up and the air was falling apart. Callie couldn't see the
flakes in the white sky. They melted in his face, in his wide
eyes. Oh, he said. Their father took him back into the house.

Callie was so white in bed. Molly read him her arithmetic
book and he learned to multiply. He didn't wear his glasses
anymore. The doctors said he could have them back in a year.
When Callie bled, Molly ran and told. Her mother and father
held ice wrapped in cloths to his nose. When they tried to lay
him out flat, Callie screamed.

Molly, her mother said. Has it stopped?

No, Molly said.

And then they felt it, warm, all over them.

Don't let my head touch down, Callie said. Don't let my head
touch down.

The last time they took him to the hospital, it was night.

Callie was wrapped tight in a blanket. It was spring it was raining it was the ambulance almost pretty in the dark. A neighbor came and stayed the night. That poor little fella, she said, had no business at the movies with his eyes so weak.

He hasn't been to the movies, Molly said. Not for a long time. He stays in bed. We only talk about the movies.

The neighbor said nothing. She stirred the hot chocolate but it burned. The scalding made a taste like dirt.

Molly's father came back and woke her up. It was almost light. He was by the window, pressing his hands on the glass. He said Callie was mighty sick; something in his head kept bleeding. They were going to the park, then to the hospital to see him.

The park was empty. By the pond, the carousel was already rusting under its pink and yellow roof. There was one black horse with its hooves in the air and its wild tongue slathering out. Her father lifted her up and put a quarter in the box. He sat on the bench. Every time Molly came around, his face was looking where she was. Her hands wouldn't move. She was crying with no sound and finally the music stopped. Her father sat on the bench in the rain with his head tilted, looking with his luminous eyes.

Satisfaction

She was my best friend, we slept together on weekends. She lived in town and I lay awake hearing her father hack in the bathroom, cars in the street passing lights on the wall. At Halloween we dressed like old men. She streaked my mouth with coal and laughed in her black teeth. Walking the south streets we hid our faces in hats and dragged one leg. Down alleys women with their hair in kerchiefs tied up garbage bags. They were only shadows against the light. We walked scratching soap on windows of the deserted bakery. I wrote those women's names. Wilhelmina, Charlotte, Vera Mae. Safety pins in their skirts and mottled cheeks. I watched them lounge against record racks in Murphey's, slanting their hard eyes at the girls in the lipstick ads.

It was cold now. Past the old bakery the houses got farther apart. Dogs howled, ran at us till chains clicked at their necks. Sudden sucked breath; they were always fooled. In a house by woods a radio blared a gospel show. Bring down the Banner my sistuhs and brothuhs. Evry road leads back to Him. Make your request and Jesus in His sweet blindness hears. An old woman nodded like a sleeper in her chair. We stood watching her through the torn screen door. Her head swiveled and she saw us in our father's hats.

Her eyes were hooded in their lids. She stood up slow, leaned on the table and the crackling radio. He is our consolation He is our light. Give us our Savior Give us our Lord. At the door she gripped the splintered frame. We held up paper bags. What? she said. What? She leaned out at us smelling cheesy as old sex. I saw we were standing in a mess on the porch. Dogs kill them rabbits, she muttered. Brings em here. Hands jerking in her hair, she faded back into the house. Her braid had come down she was twisting it her shawl dropped. In blue light she stood moving stick arms in her long dried hair. Let thou Holy hands lift up. Do not be Ashamed to hear. She forgot us. She felt for the table. He can quench the fire in your hearts He. She fumbled her hands into a bowl of butter, held them out smeared. Then calm she combed them through her hair. She tilted her head like a girl at a dance and waited to be asked. Do not doubt my sistuhs Rise. And Take the Lord in your arms. God is all over you.

I crouched by the window, drew my white X on the glass. Your soul is forged in His fire Yes He can satisfy. Inside, the old woman moaned like a wind at a door.

Country

We went down there because she was easy. She was always easy, watching us later across the stubbled field, dried-out West Virginia winter and she stood by the window braiding that long swatch of hair that smelled of smoke and fruit, of burnt apples. Sixteen, she was sixteen, moving on you, rolling flat and hard against you like some aging waitress. Feeling that hard scissored grip, you smelled her mechanical musk; her mouth on your face opened and her soft sounds spilled out empty and sugared in that filthy room. Her sheets were gray with men's dust, heavy black dust of the tunnels, and sweats mixed on her skin.

Shifts changed, that long empty whistle howling like a dog. Wizard dog, empty whirling dog. The light was flat, broken on

the hills. We walked to the truck and burned up that dirt road
to her house. House so close the mine she heard that doggy
moan and waiting for us on the porch, knife in her hand, she
peeled potatoes around and around. Eyed skins dropping limp
and curled on faded boards. She thin-legged in her man's boots.
Budded breasts and that dark, high-boned face. Mouth petulant
but its hardness in it, behind it. Looking at that mouth you felt
her teeth in you, hard white negroid teeth, and the town looked
on the whole family as niggers. This in '59, dark beauties
taunted in schools. In that old brick school on dented river
land, governor's picture in the hall smelled of river sop and the
dark tiger-eyed were taunted as they are, I guess, still, in those
towns. She had that gaunt full-hipped Appalachian stance till
she opened those lips and spoke, moving in flimsy cotton
dresses, her voice singsong like she was sleeping. She moving
smooth-bellied in fields, swell-thighed, and the harsh nettled
grass gone bleached behind her.

He, Billy, found her first. Said she was down at the company
store with her pap and a string of brats. Said she was standing
sucking her scarf, them hauling those thirty-pound bags of sta-
ples to the truck. Flour filmed in her napped hair and he said
he like to burn up looking at her. Billy and me came down from
Youngstown when the mills closed. For months I watched Billy
grind at pouty women in gritted Ohio bars, us working those
hot mills too long, going lean in a nothing town. Him a city boy
working steel and ships, tired of going back broke to married
girl friends, Lower East Side sweat-handed girls afraid of their
dock-worker husbands. Said he had an uncle, mine boss in the
South, and when the mills laid off we came down in his truck,
me having sold my junk car to get him out of jail. Drunken Billy

ended his good-bye bender smashing windows and the jaws of
some fat Puerto Rican pimp. We rolled all night into no-man's-
land West Virginia, and gas pumps alone by the side of the road
went gray. Winter then. Deserted early-morning towns dusted
gauzy; wooden-eyed perpetual thirties and Mail Pouch barns.
This ain't the South, Billy muttered, hung over, his head in his
arms on the steering wheel, This is the goddamn past. And
passing, just passing through, rolls you like a smoke train.
Those heaped mountains lower the sky and roll you like some
slow-limbed heavenly whore. And she, Billy said, that day at
the store, carried bags a man would feel. Her face was hard and
passive, the sensual hard of those women. He looked at her,
thinking *half-breed* and sexual tales. She knew it, seeing him
look as men look.

Her pap worked the Century mine down at Hundred,
worked the swing shift. Billy said he stood in the woods at the
edge of their fifteen acres of farm, waited, watched him swing
his pail and hat up the seat of that broken bed truck. Truck
started up and her pap just sat there in the shaking cab, a
brawny-armed man near fifty touching his sandy hair. Billy said
he watched him there so long he forgot the girl in the house.
Something about the way he only sat, fingers edging his face.
They lived, she told us later, in Detroit a few years when he
tried to leave the mines. Said he came home from the Chevy
plant stretched tight those nights. She cooked whatever she
could get for the kids, his woman having left him by then.
The mines, he told her, has got that dust settled in you and the
black in your gut down deep. You work in small light to tear the
wall, chink it out, then suddenly comes the monster clack of
the cars. And when they're gone, coal-heavy, the picks make the

same hard ticking up and down the rails, ticking the muffled
black. In Detroit that factory city oil smelled all night, motors
on the assembly line going till there's no rest from it. Nothing
has a weight there on the line. Just smooth whir of motors in
your head. He told her this, kneading his big hands, late nights
drunk in their neon-windowed place. Touching her, saying,
Them lines gets tight, thin cat gut lines like ties off bellies.
Them workers in line by the belts got such nothing in their
chests, after a while even the black coal dust, stealing air, is a
relief. That way he could see, he said, his years leaving him—at
least he could feel them going. He felt it mornings in his broken
truck, listening. Hounds bayed the light and field smoke rose
off the frost. The truck caught low and rumbled and he in the
shaking cab touched his face. Like something pulled his hand
and its laced black cuts to his face.

Her mother was mulatto but she was gone. The grandmother,
sometimes crazy, turned circles in the floor. We heard her outside the bedroom door, chanting, or she walked through the
house holding eggs in her hands. Old woman at the foot of the
bed motioning us to come butta butta butta. She talked non-
sense but all of them, seven kids and others drifted in from up
and down the road, they watched her. Some days, boiling jim-
son in a pot, she hung wild dope in a shed they'd used to
keep hogs. Shit walked to a powder on the warped floor. She
walked sometimes all day back and forth. Billy laughed, called
her Ole Lady Mindbender. Hey looka that, he said, his thin lips
curled, and she traced eights in the air. Gnarled fingers jabbing
close, she cackled. I kept seeing their faces together, the old
woman and the girl. The old woman cackling and she, young,

with her beige Negro face, had those same gold-irised eyes, but paler against her dark skin.

Later she talked of her thin brown mother leaving those mines her pap worked, him a doghole miner then, so poor his wife took three of the kids and went to D.C. They rode buses, riding to bars where her mother sang for hamburgers and band's donations. Finally she whored out of Baltimore hotels, the kids waiting outside on the stoop. Ten-dollar tricks and swarthy short-order cooks. Movie house janitors' nicotined fingers and doughy thighs of the satin-haired dago cops. Most nights the kids slept below in alley porno shop, warmer there, and Baker, black faggot, kept mattresses in back. Baker, his moony bagged eyes, his old bottles in windows, gave them white gravy and bread at 3 A.M. Alley feet stumbled by his grilled basement windows, size of tomato boxes. It was '49 and he talked about the war, hiding his knobby hands. Sunk easy in a flushed barbiturate high, he gave the kids Japanese fans GIs had traded for pinups. Filmy cataracts liquid as spaniel's eyes, he said he 'got to move dis place up da street, up dere woan hafta burn dese lights all day.' She and her brothers stole opiated cough syrup he heated in a pan. They stole tuna and steak from the grocery and they ate good some days, upstairs not so cold come spring. Then it was hot, so hot they breathed their own sweat. Their mother laughed, broad mouth stretched tight, eating on carton table in empty grime city rooms. Fans on full, she wore a bra and panties, fed them beer and fried meat. Brown woman, her black hair kerchiefed or pulled back in a knot. High-cheeked opal face, thick-browed, her smell raw in rooms. The heat that summer, and at the hotel there was backed-up plumbing, sad junkies on the roof, hot-summer Baltimore hepatitis. Their mother taken from mattress on floor no talking. At the crowded hospital, they were separated, beds or different floors, white wards, and she, seven years old, though it was because someone knew they had stolen the food. She and the brother left were sent back to the country, where their father had a woman, more sons.

She had an older brother at Moundsville, sent up I guess for car theft, big-time state-pen theft. She wrote him letters on schoolgirl's lined paper, careful not to smudge pencil sketches of the hounds she kept for him. Billy making her laugh would kiss the dogs passionate, holding them tackled in his arms until she ran to him. The dogs jumped, yelping their womanish sounds. Working with her pap on their truck, we drank Dickel and the dogs, five big loose hounds, nuzzled our hands with their pink snouts. Billy went back to town in the late evening. The rest of them left through the woods to the mission church where the grandmother spoke in tongues and translated what they called the Word. That full-mooned night her pap and me had the engine out in the quiet. We worked together and the church sounded faint through the trees, a distanced animal music come to echo by the house. Don't like my kids going, he said. It's hypnosis, some part don't no one need see. And the women raving, he said, Jesus no lover for a woman. He said it low, corners of his mouth gone soft, his hard face naked. He looked at me, and I thought for the first time that he must have been with her, not now, but long before, and more than once. He seeing me know stood confused and then brought his big arms down fisted. We rolled in the yard and I felt her in hi

arms in that Detroit room. I tried to say it was all right, I
thought she would be all right, but I hit him because he wanted
me to. He wanted to be hit, beaten, but he came at me so hard
I fell under him, then saw his brutal face go sad. We said
nothing, sat there in patched snow.

Toward spring, Billy left for the last time. Billy in New York
with his East Side girls laughed no doubt then seriously talked
of this cool-faced girl in her miner father's house. You're the
good boy here, he told me. I go, he said, you stay. When I first
went there alone (that is, everything was changed), we stood in
the yard. She feeding chickens made a ck ck ck sound, sucking
her cheeks. I watched her lips move, feeling oddly freaked
there in the mud yard near the scraggly chickens and their
round soulless eyes. Their washed yellow beaks were faded and
sharp and her mouth moved, talking them close with some
gentle sexual sound. I felt like I'd never slept with her, like
both of us, Billy and me, had really only watched her, watched
her strange small house and the dirt-scratched farm in big
fields, watched the crouched mountains. At first it was like she
said, no one around here going anywhere. Then things started
moving, sliding; she got to us. When she talked, her curved-
edged words ran together, her voice coming low in her throat.
There in the yard, early daylight flattened space between us.
Seemed I'd never seen her in such light. Always before it was
pale. Subdued winter midnights till 6 A.M., the one big bed.
Coal stove going and kids asleep in the house. One or two up in
the night came in to sleep with us, whimpering. Billy got up
first and sat in the chair, reading Revelations out loud drunk-
enly to himself and she slept close to me. I watched windows in

by-then late winter, trees wobbly and the shack buildings pale
through the plastic-covered windows.

Or I saw her in dim lights, warm, like in the pool hall in town
those afternoons, dark, and the balls cracking sides under one
low light hung from ceiling. She on flat stool by the bar talked
maybe to Lowry, the owner, whose breath smelled always of
black beans, whom she knew well, having helped his old lady
midwife in the county since she was a kid. Solemn by steaming
cunts of cousins and her father's women, she held pans for the
hamlike hands of Elva Lowry. Telling me later (long after
chickens in cold spring), once they went clear to Pickens in
Elva's Ford, a not-bright woman whooing like a cow for two
days. Her one-armed man in the kitchen yelled Shut that up
now, and finally the baby birthed breech. Elva, sweating,
wrapped it, he frying fat in a shallow pan in the kitchen where
she went to wash it. Elva was gone and the woman blathered
about jams, about crookberries. Get out there at the pump now,
Elva said. Get water, ain nobody finished here. Another baby
came. It was blue, its head dented. Elva laid it down. There,
she said, let the poor thing go. Women, she said, got the sense
of camels.

In the poolroom Lowry told stories. Elva, he said, was a
good doctor till she died her own self. Ain't that the way. He
laughed in the rosy light and wiped glasses with a rag. Behind
him the cheap beer signs threw shadows and made his head big
on the wall. In that light she was easy to look at, her crossed
legs shiny in dollar nylons, her head bent in her hair. Making a

shot she never smiled, just chalked her stick and waited. Billy
guzzled cold beer and sharpened in the fuzzy room. He sharpened, his face seemed clearer in those half-lights (he said to
me in private even then, I got to get out of this). Afterward
we'd give her a ride to her place with the groceries. The town
looked abandoned with its slope-roofed buildings, even old men
on stoops sat alone. Those late afternoons everyone was gone to
the mines or to the Carbide plant. Me and Billy full of male
laughter told tales, entertaining her but really gaming each
other. She scratched her nails slow on the coarse bags in her
lap. Billy, mock serious, said he was going to paint this truck in
red letters, name it The Triangle. The whole truck smelled of
him and beer. His shirt open he howled Hoo Whee, the ped-
dler the priest and the miner's daughter. She laughed, all of us
suddenly sweating. That spring turned hot before he left. He
poured cold beer down his neck, in his hair, saying Why does
he have to drive this bus Why the hell does he always have to
drive. She said Why Billy because you're the only one got sense
enough not to ask questions. All of us got drunk on beer and
Cutty Sark and then lay in the creek to sober in cold water.

She told me later (Billy running coke in the Bowery, heisting
TVs in sad-faced apartments for bucks) she'd heard Billy talking.
She said sometimes he'd get so drunk she'd find him in the
woods outside the house, unconscious, open-eyed, unable to
move and mumbling terrified about avenues and sharks. Early
spring in the yard that morning it was still cool but the sun was
a glassy promised heat. Billy's eyes were gone but they were
close—I felt them in her dress, where she held feed aproned in
the cloth, her sounding ck ck ck and the stupid staccato chickens. Going in the house she tripped, the chickens clouding her

feet. She called one of the kids in from the woods. He was the
youngest, the rest were in school by then. Bubby, she yelled.
Come on back here. But he stood still in the yellow field. We
started for him and he came, dragging what we thought was
rope but as he came closer we saw it was a big blacksnake gap-
ing its harmless mouth. He held it up and we saw its eggs
rounded under the hide. He touched its end on the ground and
an egg eased out on the grass. The snake, elastic around the
shell, tried to coil. The boy looked at us, seemed to forget the
snake and left it there on the steps. She stared at it in a way
that scared me. I pulled her into the kitchen and she began
filling up every pan and kettle in the house with water. The
old woman caught on and hauled buckets from the pump.
The kid, crowing, hitched up his pants and ran, following her,
scuttling in the dirt. The woodburning stove was fired up and
thickened the air. The sun got hotter, rubbing on the glass. We
opened windows and doors, both of us seeing the swollen snake
still on the porch. We moved the big tub to the center of the
floor and she burned her hands lugging the heavy kettles. I
moved behind her to take them and pressed against her by the
wooden tub. The water steamed and I felt her skin under flan-
nel. She was so familiar, the granted smell of her, the dark hay
smell. Seeing her firm full-lipped face, I was frightened again
by the old stare in her eyes as she'd watched the snake, her
stare as she'd watched pitted windows in Billy's rainy truck.
Stopping for gas the day before he left, we'd talked past her and
she watched numbers turn on the pumps. Listened. Harsh rake
of the nozzle, clunk of its handling.

I got in the water with her, the big tub smelling of soaked
pine. The old woman turned garden outside and the woods

were overgrown already (was it April?). We bathed each other, soaped her black-nippled breasts, and the little boy between us was slippery, shivering against us. She rose, dripping water. The wet floor was shaded dark. She wrapped the boy in blankets and put him in a chair. All of it, everything, so slow. Seeming we are in the water for hours, her kinky hair pasted to her back and face in tight curls, she stepping over dogs asleep on the damp floor and me dreaming of us alone in some Southwest, some Canada. She dried me with her hands in bed, her mouth on my eyes. Kunk of old woman's hoe at the side of the house. We had each other slow, looking at ourselves. Like when he and I came from the mine that first time she took our clothes, put her face to our white stomachs. We drank cheap hot whiskey, kissed her whiskied mouth and she laughed. Our black faces rubbed her shoulders gray. And it gets confused, she, her face on me, silent, oh god easing into her we're in the dark.

Slave

She wanted to have orgasms more and more often. She watched her men have orgasms with their eyes closed, sailing on their breath, and gone. She had the pleasure of helping them leave, and was left in possession of them until they returned. She had memorized faces in that moment of unconsciousness. Many times she was actually seeing that face rather than the face she was talking to, aware that this person whose face it was had never seen that face of himself. So the face became her secret. She herself had a tiny orgasm of fear when she saw someone she loved after a long separation, who usually no longer loved her. Something turned over once in her. She had the same turning ache when reading something suggestive or having a memory of arousal. She had it when she realized she wanted someone.

When she masturbated she always had a brief intense orgasm, turning over ten times, and fell asleep released. But she seldom had orgasms with her men. She loved to make love with some-one she wanted. They soared away from her arched and para-lyzed and for an instant she had what she wanted. There was one man she liked to talk to, whom she didn't particularly want because he was so much like her. She already had what he had. She could get along without him, because when he came, there was no triumph of conquering their separation and winning him. So she told him that although she liked men she seldom had orgasms with them but only with herself. They talked about it patiently. After that she wanted to make love with him less because her power was exposed and solidified. He wanted to make love with her more but was self-conscious because he was unsure of his power. She felt he was no longer like her but was less than her, and she didn't want him. The relationship cooled. One day he called her on the phone and a fight ensued in which they each cataloged what was weak about the other. She was getting the best of him so he said Go fuck yourself, since you can do more for yourself than I can anyway. She sat there listen-ing to the dial tone. She knew that he thought her power was uppermost because she could make him come but he couldn't make her come. He had the secret of what her power was about, but she had the secret of his powerlessness over her. That made him ashamed. He felt lonely but free because he thought there had to be two people to have the question of power. She knew her power over him happened because of her power over herself. The phone began bleeping frantically. Alone, she could feel her power holding her up. But what did that make her?

Accidents

I'm not sure anymore when the first accident happened. Or if it was an accident. Now when I tell you about my accidents you are sympathetic and some of you fall in love with me. Men whose childhoods were slow and smooth want my straitjacket stories. My sugar is a panic that melts on your tongue and leaves a tiny hole in what you taste. Taste me Sugar, I'm fried around the edges. Mom used to say I was born with my eyes crossed. That was a joke she quit telling when I was old enough and wrapped up tight. You feel me spinning and the music's on too loud. You remember all the little dangers in your past. My body that long sleek car someone spun on curves, Hey you wanna drag? Yeah I'll do ya, and it degenerates. Six girls giggly drunk jumping out to run circles around an old Chevy at a red light. Hey wait a minute Honey, you dropped somthin. I keep dropping how things went, which story goes where. This week and next week and next week. Somewhere out there's a winner but I'm losing track. I try to stay home and turn the pages in my books. But the words are a dark crusted black that cracks. Black as wine or water. I keep wading out and the deep part is over my head. I wanna dance I wanna just wrap my legs around you like those rings are round the moon. Lemme press my mouth against you like the rain against the glass it's see-through. I can see clear out there to the end and I'm alone I'm burning like a fire fuel. I'm hot. I'm hot I'm a streak across the sky. You watch me, now bring me down hard and hold on. It doesn't matter if I tell one truth or another. I wanna feel a hand on my waist. He and I are through, why don't you come over? See, I hurt my head again. I hit it on the bed.

Gemcrack

She is sitting in the car and I do my number. Looking down the sight I see an aureole flare to the right and left, all around in haloed flutters. Then it wavers like underwater noons, I have to split, my Uncle doesn't wait. He says be back, be quick, be reverent. We pray for these great states, for the Great State of the City of New York. We make em break em cart em away, Zing! like a silver cat scratch burning way down where you recognize your name. I make a sound: the letter S, snakes leaving skin to sun. Her head sinks down; I hear the sound and right away I'm fluttering. Gem-stepping down the alley I turn, squeeze off a quick shot and the girl half dazed on sidewalk falls over, lays down like she's home. And I'm running, rolling round like the eyes of Jesse James. Love is the outlaw's duty.

You see me everywhere. I spit on the surface of night, on the
rattling backdrops of subway gutter art. I suck you up like eras-
ers. I am that glittering drop of mercury spilled out a broken
glass stick. Mark me in numbers and names of the dead. I take
your temperature, your pulse. I have my fingers on your wrist
and I will twist it. You suppose I fade as my women fade,
buried or barricaded; my women with their swinging hair and
their protectors. But no, I am with you though you walk
through the lit-up noise of Mondays; I comfort you. I know the
accountant's language of knuckles and swivel chairs, the jostling
streets, the department store blues of floorwalkers and lyric
radios, the sweat of the laundress scheming in powders and
starch, the burger joints deemed blessed by girls in their thin
white legs. I love my work. I crack these gems and expose their
light in the dark Saturdays, the nights. My Uncle leads me
astray into the paths of right thoughts. He holds my hand. Wait,
he says, the time is not right—but we will yet have what we
need. And surely, what we need comes in its time.

I read the papers. I save the stories in a box. They print my
letters to the press, my exhortations to action. Get off your col-
lective ass and rise to the occasion, rattle doors, knock on the
deafened tombs. Haunt the alleys of the city which shine with
slivered glass and clues to the underside. Inspect the eyes of
winos. Inspect bellies in rotten shirts beached up on curbs,
heads cradled stupid in a pasty arm. The whores, the Catholic
girls, speak well of these whales of the streets. They sit on
lumps of sleeping flesh to wait for a bus or a trick. They keep
their jewels in trash cans and adorn themselves by the light of
the moon. The drunks, the sleeping whales, have seen it pass.
Ask these prophets where I lie in wait, where I sleep to evade
your manhunters in their uniforms and carbolic faces. Ask the
prophets whose shaggy heads slumber on newsprint fantasies of

my face, on news of the latest sacrifice. I live in the gutters of dog manure, wine and urine; in the sewers which eat these melodies delivered by the sprays of the sweeper trucks.

Remember Babylon. I live in a swelter of bobbing heads navigating east and west far down in the streets. I ride the elevators up sixty floors; I stand at the windowed corner of a big hotel on a forgotten floor. Alone in a hallway while the rows of locked doors sleep, I watch the swelter break and sigh. The swelter rolls like waves; an ocean of passengers on foot. Watch it move. Beneath me, far down in the streets, the ocean wobbles in red shoes and three-piece suits. Those red shoes! wooden heels stacked in layers of light and dark like a parquet floor dismantled and cut to fit. Ankles above the shoes are strung thin and tuned to recite. Though I see only tops of heads, female heads smaller than the metal caps of straight pins, I remember the ankles: their nylon sheen, the round bones rising up to glint like a covered eye.

Once I shot marbles. Glass and porcelain. Agates. Colors snaked in stripes through the centers, formed a wavered pupil of no determined expression. Handfuls of lovely eyes. I propelled one with my thumb to hit others, drive them out of a circle scratched on the ground. I crouched with the rest. I crouched in my scarred shoes and took aim. I dented my shoes on rocks and sticks. Those shoes were brown and tied with long ties which tangled or dragged in the dirt. Gouged scratches in the leather turned pale and tempered like scars on skin. I dug my fingernails into the dirt and aimed. We played marbles on the hard-packed ground, dust baked blond in the sun. I kept my prizes in a string bag. Scooping up the captive jewels, I rolled them in my hands and kept them warm. Later I would examine them by a light, sit home alone and stare into their centers. Now the boys crowded round with smears of dirt on

their faces, silent, while the high-pitched screams of girls sig-
naled they were sweating at their games of tag. Girls ran close
and teased us with the sounds of their buckled sandals. Slaps on
the ground. Quick. Flat. No one looked. The boys watched me,
my cat's-eye. Its chatoyant luster glimmered onto my skin: a
stripe of shade burned in.

Shade falls on me as I walk among the faces. I walk east and
west with my hands in my pockets. By day the discos are only
the flat mutes of their doors and lightless signs. The crowd flows
past them. Some of us walk in the black slant. A shadow falling
from a long place is cast across us. Perhaps we will meet at
night, in an alley beside a club. They sit in a parked car. They
see me, some stand and sink. As they fall off their shoes I
remember my own, those scarred leather ones with rounded
toes. Was my Uncle watching me then, in my crouch? My cat's-
eye shot in its spinning roll across the dirt, rolled with its chosen celebrant beyond the scratched circle into no-man's-land.
Listen: I'll discuss my country; the playgrounds of the Bronx
where buildings hedge their sooty roofs together and the
dented rain pipes glitter. The ground was littered with smashed
bottles. We ate Push-Ups, slender creamsicles frozen to a stick.
We bought them across the street from the school for a dime.
The sticks were saved, sharpened with penknives, used in
games of pirates.

The girls and boys. We evaded each other. No one wanted
the secrets yet, just the surging underskin like splinters. Some
days it rained. They kept us inside. Ceilings of the classrooms
were high and cracked. Above us in a heavy frame hung a por-

trait of George Washington in clouds, his patrician nose rouged
and tipped with a ball of light. Each morning we recited the
Pledge. Then the prayer about the hollow Father and the coming Kingdom, the heavenly Will. My Uncle grinned in my mind
but kept silent. He saved his commands and watched me. In
the rain the old school building smelled of chalk and dirt. Dirt
rubbed into the floor and packed itself firmly in cracks. We dug
it up with pencil tips. Outside, the grounds were gray. Swings
moved on chains. The teacher left us alone for recess. She
snuck cigarettes in a lounge with a closed door; she thought of
nothing. Noise in the classroom got louder and louder. The girls
made games and diversions. Some wore full dresses with crino-
line slips, ankle socks, patent leather shoes. They stood inside
the reading circle and twirled to records of rhymes. Goosey
Goosey Gander, whither shall I wander? Upstairs and downstairs and in my lady's chamber. There I met an old man who
would not say his prayers. I took him by the left leg and threw
him down the stairs . . . The girls twirled, seeing how big their
skirts became. I lay on the floor inside the circle of chairs.
Above me the skirts volumined like umbrellas. I saw the girl's
legs, thin and coltish. Pale. The ankle socks chopped their
calves above the ankle and gave the illusion of hooves. I saw
their odd white pants and their flatness. They were clean like
dolls. They smelled of powder. They flashed and moved. I turned
my face to the hard blond legs of the chairs.

At night I wake up. I put my hands across my face but the
smell persists. My fingers smell of onions. I want to peel back
the skin layer by layer, find the smell and wash it. I smell of

something cut up, limp curls on boards, limp curled skins of onions.

My Uncle says, Come close. He stands in the shadows by the window. He stands behind the long curtains and ripples the dirty cloth. I see his shoes sticking out beneath, laced-up military boots and green woolen socks on his ankles. Come, he says. I see his head moving behind the cloth. He is unkind when he is angry. He is waiting for me to get on with the work. He comes at me out of everyone's mouth until I know he is the only one talking. He's inside the hippie across the hall with the moon poster tacked to his door, inside the black girls I see in the elevator. They say Hi, they taunt me with their sloe-fizzed eyes and the pinkish palms of their hands. My Uncle waits at night in the dark bedroom until I wake up and listen. Come close to me, he says. And then he begins the giggling, long idiot sounds drawn out warbling and buckling, drawn out circling to choke me.

I have a job in the days. Always on time. Holding my computer card to the time clock, I hear a magic click writing numbers. The clock has a face of cats and rats; a black-ringed face with hands like whiskers. I like to check sizes, work in the stock shelves. I pull a folding ladder along the shelves, between the endless rows. Rows and rows of shoe boxes stacked to the ceiling, printed in size and swirled calligraphy; Spectator, Top o' the Town, Mr. Rocker. Mr. Rocker shoes are spangled with mirrors on clear plastic heels, sewn in satin stripes, dappled with brass studs. Girls paint their toenails red and go dancing in Mr. Rockers. They sway on their transparent platforms while

the music bleats. Mostly they don't move their feet; they bend
at the waist, side-to-side, arch hips and slinky strut. They close
their eyes. Smile. Others stamp their feet, beat time with Mr.
Rockers, pound sequined heels the width of a peg leg. I know
because I go to watch them. My Uncle stands beside me; he
whispers and points. He tells me what to do in his voice that
whines and excites, his old voice that talks in the eyes of the
reeling prophets and clattering cans in the streets. He knows
languages with no letters. When he sees Mr. Rockers glitter
under strobes, he grips my arm and buzzes like a bee.

But now I watch the escalators, shoes on the moving steps.
They pass up and down, back and forth in front of our department. The manager rubs his hands and nods. I have a silver
shoehorn in my pocket. When no one comes in, sits in our
enclave of padded chairs, I dust shelves of Mr. Rockers with a
feather duster. The salesgirls sit and saw their nails with emery
boards embossed in the name of the franchise. They wear sensi-
ble shoes, beige Wedgies and Weejuns with pennies. They are
required to wear stockings and shoes with covered toes. Their
ankles are shy and crossed with a strap. I could show them
places to go. My Uncle nods. He is serious about my work; only
I can serve him in my way.

By late afternoon the store slows down. The empty escalators
move. Women at the jewelry counters lean on the glass, looking
closely at rows of pierced earrings. But they aren't really looking, only flicking at dangling golds with a fingernail. They're
thinking of catching buses, eating dinner, locking their doors to
sleep. And the accountants walk by, hurried, lace slips for wives
tucked in a briefcase. The days get darker. The lawyers, deli
owners, insurance salesmen, aging girls from publishing houses:
they fill up subway cars and stare straight ahead. They remark
on the newspapers. Some save clippings, fascinated. At the

stalker, the legions of manhunters, the series of chosen faces innocent in those painful graduation pictures. I know which
readers follow the stories. Their faces are looking for secrets.
I'm pushing them. I could tell them light comes in one quick
flash to the seeker.

The apartment was always dim. The Bronx was rows of tene-
ments, metal fire escapes at spindled angles, thin grass strips by
lengths of sidewalk. Junked cars in the street. Basketballs made
their repetitive rubber slaps on pavement. My mother worked a
factory in Brooklyn; she rode the trains home late. We were
alone in the place. Every night I waited for her. We kept a
wooden crate by the door, a steel door like the rest with a two-
inch-square window high up. I stood on the crate to watch for
her, a short wirehaired woman lumbering in kerchief and
shapeless dress up the stairs. She always carried groceries. She
said she liked my eyes right there at the window after she'd
climbed three flights with the heavy bag. So I pushed the crate
to the door and watched. One rectangular light in the hall cast a
yellow shape on the floor. I stood there for hours. I watched
them all come and go.

Daughters of the Spanish family across the hall folded clothes
at the Laundromat. They were dark and brassy, gold hoops in
their ears, wrinkled cigarettes. They came home after five and
fumbled with keys, shifting big purses and bundles of towels
bound with a paper strip. In the warm box of light their faces
lost sharp expression, seemed rounder, tawny. They all had
moles near their lips, dark little pigments ignored and sexual.
The dark spots rose like tiny scarabs on their faces. The girls

tossed their heavy black hair. They sighed, shifted hips, jingled their rings of gold keys. They were sleepwalkers slouched by the metal doors. I wanted to wake them up.

And there were others, all asleep, all waiting. Fat women who worked in the markets, cleaning women, women who did nothing. Men came back with their silver lunch pails. Most of them lived alone or transient. Their faces were putty in the light. Only the shamblers, the rocking drunks, didn't care. They yelled and pounded on doors, walked into walls and laughed. Their stubbled whiskers gleamed. They opened their mouths wide and threads of spit glistened like dewed web. I believed they had spiders inside them. They were the only ones: they saw my eyes at the window. They pointed at me. They bowed, doffed their lumpy hats, and fell down in a heap.

Mostly I'm invisible. I stay in my apartment. I go to work and come home. In summer I turn off the air-conditioner and open windows. I like to feel it all heat up. The city gets hotter and hotter. Tar bubbles on roofs and tops of cars shine white. The air gets heavy and hums. Suddenly, when its hardest to breathe, sirens cut loose. The heat is punctured like a big bag; the weight leaks out and whines. Ambulances or fire trucks. Or cops. Long sirens blurring in and out, screaming to make things real. I sit still. After the sirens there will be sounds again; doors slammed, strays barking in the streets. Colors start in the sky and night comes on. I hear footsteps in the hall. My Uncle is walking around. His sounds are in my head like a voice in a radio.

* * *

My mother said to stay inside. She said those sleeping drunks in the halls would steal my clothes. I counted marbles I'd won and left the best ones out to show her. The Bronx smelled of garbage left in a heat, smelled of a whole city wasting. I watched the electric fans revolve their whirring heads. I turned off the lights and watched them in the dark; the glinting circles they made.

When my mother got home we played cards. Crazy Eights or Slapjack. She was quick at slapping Jacks. Her hand came down hard on their faces, their jeweled capes, their little hatchets. She wore no rings; her nails were blunt-cut straight across. After she'd won all the cards she shuffled the deck and dealt us hands of eight. Sometimes she let me win. I changed suits to hearts or diamonds, neat red shapes: I still see them when I look at neon signs. My mother smoked Pall Malls and took the combs out of her hair. She was always old. She rolled down her heavy support stockings, rubbed lotion on her calves. She rubbed gingerly at places where the dark blue veins were coming up, as if she were afraid of her insides. She told me twice she never knew my mother. Other times she'd say how sick she'd been when I was born.

Once we heard a shuffling in the hall, snarls and squeaks. One of the alley dogs had got in and caught a rat. The dog had it by the throat and their eyes were wild, wide open, rolling. I called her to look and she grabbed me. She pulled me back from the door, from the window that fit my eyes. She held me to the opposite wall and stood shivering while the sounds went on. She kept her hands on my neck. I looked up from beneath her and saw her parted lips, the edges of her teeth. And her eyes had sharp edges to them, watching the metal door.

* * *

Each time, I do the same things. I come home and lock the locks. I have a mattress on the floor and a box of clippings. I read them over and over and listen for his voice. It starts coming every night; my Uncle is there all the time. I go for weeks and then it is time again. I take the gun out and look at it.

When I went in the army my mother cooked a big dinner. She fried chicken and mashed the potatoes. She stood cooking gravy, stirring it with a fork. The skin of her arms was cracked and crossed with tiny lines. She thought the army would be good for me: I could go to school on the GI Bill. I watched her standing at the stove. She wore white waitress shoes with thick soles and she had a big safety pin fastened to the collar of her dress. She saved rubber bands, paper clips, thumbtacks, safety pins. When she found them in the apartment she put them in a pocket or fastened the pins to her clothes. She stirred the bubbling gravy and hummed hymns. By then her face was pasty and she wheezed. She hummed "We Gather Together." The army, she said, maybe I'd be an engineer. Design machines and engines. I'd always been smart, she said, why shouldn't I have the best.

At Fort Dix I was a typist. I hated the khaki uniforms. I hated the southern boys and their jokes. They only noticed me when they told their dirty stories. If I didn't laugh they said I needed a whore. They came close to my face and their little pig eyes glittered through slits.

I learned how to shoot. I practiced. I shot at clip-on targets printed in red and yellow rings. The black bull's-eye spiraled

deep. I hit it and dreamed of hitting it. In dreams I laced up my
boots and walked in the dark to the target range. I saw each
step and when I touched the gun I saw through the bones of my
hands. I kept shooting into the eye of the black and a star burst
up each time. At first I didn't notice the girls. Then, one by
one, they started filtering out of the woods; slim girls in knee-
length dresses whose bare arms stayed still as they walked.
They walked slow, their hair billowed out. They stood dotting
the meadow and gazed at me like waiting deer. I kept shooting.
Stars in the black bull's-eyes burst brighter and brighter. The
girls stayed motionless, their faces toward me. The sky grew
lighter above their pale dresses. Their feet were hidden in
grasses. Across the rolling field their arms gave off faint glows.

I wait for a weekend. Saturday night. All day I wait for the
dark. My Uncle is with me though he is not present.

I look at the gun and I touch it. I turn it over and touch it everywhere. I have everything I need and his voice has stopped
and I go where his voice has said to go. I park the car and I walk
a few blocks. I have the gun in my pocket and the note I have
signed for his voice. I don't wonder about the girl; I'll read
about her later, her parents, where she lived, what she did.
Now she is dancing or she is getting smoke in her eyes from the
cigarettes in the crowded room and she is getting ready to walk
outside. I hear a buzzing and my vision flickers. In an alley by
the side entrance of the club I have my hand ready; I see her
hair and her red coat. Sometimes they don't see me but she
does and that's good, it's very good; because she shakes me, I'm
fluttering, she rushes in like electric shock in the instant she
looks at me and knows—I never hear the gun—But after she
falls there is a loud crack. Something big caves in. The white-

ess comes up brilliant, sudden, stutters sparks and spreads its
burning arms. Then a flash like imploding air. I pass through
like flame. My shoes bleach concrete where I touch. Sometime,
someone will see and follow me. I'll say they found me with
special eyes; I'll say they have grown up in light.